THEA lay rigid, her ears straining for the sound, or whatever it was that had wakened her, certain in her mind that she had not dreamed it. No! There it was again! A furtive scrabbling.

Instinctively she reached for her robe and eased open the door. She headed for the stairway and began to climb.

Suddenly she was aware of a muted thump as some part of the ceiling, so it seemed, was flung back, and then a storm lanthorn from an open trap door above her flashed full on her upturned face. Behind it, an unidentifiable shape crouched and then, on the sight of her, gave a furious cry and, leaving the lanthorn above, leapt forward and down, a swirling mass of dark cloak and clutching hands. . . .

Fawcett Crest Books
by Joan Mellows:

A DIFFERENT FACE 24046-0 $1.75

A FAMILY AFFAIR 22967-X $1.50

FRIENDS AT KNOLL HOUSE P2530 $1.25

HARRIET 23209-3 $1.50

A DIFFERENT FACE

Joan Mellows

FAWCETT CREST • NEW YORK

A DIFFERENT FACE

Published by Fawcett Crest Books, a unit of CBS
Publications, the Consumer Publishing Division of
CBS Inc.

ISBN: 0-449-24046-0

Printed in the United States of America

10   9   8   7   6   5   4   3   2   1

A
DIFFERENT
FACE

Chapter 1

THEA, at twenty-six, was considered an unusual woman; at seventeen, she had been considered an unusual young girl; and before that, an unusual child. Though this was never meant in a derogatory fashion, still it was not always complimentary. Some said it with awe, some with amusement, and a few close friends, with very warm affection. Although extremely pretty, and now turning into a rather severe beauty, she had not only a quick intelligence, but was also disconcertingly well educated, for her father was one of those strange beings who felt that women had as much right to the mysteries of Latin, Greek, and even mathematics, should they wish it, as men. Thea was an only child, and her mother, although the nicest and most unexceptionable of women, had been so featherbrained as not even to realize where such an excess of erudition might lead her daughter. Mr. Langham had therefore had his way and instructed his daughter himself, in his own scholarly fashion. Fortunately, Thea's temperament was equable and her affections warm. She had always liked people; and the childhood parties and, later, the balls and routs, all the social life her family's position inevitably entailed, she enjoyed to the full. Moreover, this interest in her fellows usually prevented her from cruelly exercising a very pretty wit, while a natural, if rather acid, sense of humor seldom allowed her to overvalue herself.

All the same, she *was* unusual, and, thus, highly endowed with both brains and beauty, rather intimidating. There was, too, perhaps naturally in the circumstances, a more serious, darker side to her nature, an awareness—from her wide reading alone—of the eternal miseries of the world, of poverty, sickness, degradation, of the frequent indignities of old age, of bereavement; of everything, in fact, on the reverse side of the coin from her own happy existence, so that her conversation was apt to be disconcerting. Still, she had learned, as she grew older, to keep such observations in the main to herself, and now, at twenty-six, had herself so well in hand as not to embarrass her companions too frequently by either her intermittent dark thoughts, or her ingrained erudition.

She had several times fancied herself to be in love, but her fiendishly inconvenient sense of humor had usually spoiled matters for her before her feelings had had time to become too intense. Young gentlemen, and even more so, older, dignified, more serious-minded ones, have a marked distaste for being laughed at when attempting to declare themselves, or even when attempting to fix their interest; even if, afterward, the object of their affections is undoubtedly contrite. Such sad fiascos had of late, however, become far less frequent. Thea had discovered, with indifference, that the unmarried men of her wide acquaintance were either too young, those her own age usually being married, or not to her taste, being either ramshackle, or conceited, or pompous, or dead bores. Indeed, she realized to her inner alarm (for she was, after all, gently reared), that the only men who did appeal to her were the cheerful, good-hearted and raffish ones, (as against the fortune hunters for whom, naturally, she had no time) or those canny enough to have escaped the marriage mart, with its complement of determined mammas.

The fact that this preference limited her already dwindling choice considerably did not worry her. She had become, in fact, completely self-sufficient, and having a well-stocked mind and a passion for reading whatever came to hand, never suffered from boredom, as did so many of her sex when they weren't gossiping, dancing or flirting. Very sensibly, those really fond of her asked themselves—and occasionally Thea herself—how she would go on when she reached the age (now not so distant) of chaperonage rather than of participation in the social pleasures she so enjoyed. But she would merely laugh and turn her pretty head, with its thick auburn hair cut fashionably short, saying lightly that she was looking forward to all the fun of the card tables (she was already an expert whist player, to the disapproval of many), and if this palled, she could perhaps write treatises on such subjects as "The Influence of the Passions on the Happiness of Individuals and of Nations," like that formidable Madame de Staël. She would never allow herself to dwell on possible future sadness but pursued her life evenly and pleasurably, without either regretting the past or fearing what was to come.

In this context, a favorite cousin, her father's sister's son, a young man of twenty, with a wit very much akin to her own, had once remarked that she was well-named Thea, and like a goddess she behaved—as though she would always control the world as her oyster. When she replied that her name was not Thea but Anthea (her father having an uncharacteristic and unfashionable love of Robert Herrick's poems), the young man had continued that it was all one, goddess or unfashionably named mortal, she would end an old maid unless she came out of the clouds and considered where her superior mind was leading her.

Such facetiousness was worth only an amusing reply, but it rankled Thea far more, in fact, than the cautious warnings of her close friends. She was considering it afresh as she walked, one bright spring day, with the fierce winter and the terrible War over, along Bruton Street after a comfortable coze with some friends and a browse in the nearby circulating library. Suddenly something hit her violently behind the right shoulder. Alarmed, (her father had often remonstrated with her, mildly, on refusing either the town carriage or her abigail's company on what he called these "book jaunts"), she half-turned in time to prevent a young girl, rather plainly clad, from falling to the ground. The newcomer, glancing hastily down the narrow passage she had so suddenly hurtled from, and apologizing in the high, distrait voice of the truly harassed, showed no sign of moving away, however, after Thea had assured her she was neither angry nor physically hurt.

Instead, her hands rather tightened on Thea's wrists, where she had caught her and asked breathlessly,

"Oh, ma'am, I beg you, could we pretend we knew each other, just for a minute?"

The question was unconventional; the young voice itself unexceptionable, unquestionably well-bred. Intrigued and moved by her usual impulsive kindness, Thea agreed and was rewarded by a look of gratitude that, while it pleased, also disquieted her. She added reassuringly,

"Though I cannot think it can matter whether we already know each other or not. I can easily come to know you *now*, can I not?"

There was no time for a reply to this. The passage suddenly echoed to heavy, running feet, and a large man, tall, well-dressed, with heavy shoulders and an arrogant tilt to his head came to a stop in front of them. Taking no notice whatever of Thea—an almost totally new experience for her—the new arrival said, a little breathlessly, to her new acquaintance,

"Come, George, we'll have no more of this foolishness. Go back to the carriage." He waved his hand imperiously toward the passage, at the far end of which, Thea now observed, was a smart closed carriage from which an elegant woman was descending hurriedly with the aid of a liveried servant.

The girl addressed so strangely as George threw an anguished glance at Thea and said, in a high, false, social voice,

"Sir, this is a friend of mine. We met at the Dillinghams'. She is Miss . . ." Her voice failed suddenly but Thea, who had already taken a perhaps unreasonable dislike to the tall, arrogant newcomer, and hearing with relief the name of a family she herself knew well, introduced herself smoothly without any noticeable pause. She was adding, for her young friend's benefit, that Maria, the eldest Miss Dillingham—now Lady Barton—was one of her greatest friends, when the elegant third member of the party appeared in what seemed to be a state of considerable agitation. She, too, ignored Thea, turning to say, in a thin, complaining voice, "Oh, you tiresome, tiresome child, what a time you give me! And to run off so, with only those thin dancing pumps on your feet—you will likely have a bad cold to answer for it!"

Thea thought she heard a small, quavery voice observe, in very low tones, what use were pumps when one never got to attend dancing class, but her elders either did not hear, or ignored this remark. The woman turned with an air of marked disapproval to Thea, and raised her thin eyebrows at her escort, who said, peremptorily,

"Miss Thea Langham. Friend of the Dillinghams. George met her there."

Cold, gray eyes assessed Thea briefly, and presumably satisfactorily, for a pinched smile flickered for a moment on the well-formed, but thin lips, and the woman put out her hand. But Thea had not been used to such ill-breeding as she had so far encountered and, moreover, her sympathies were far more with poor George than with her elders, who were obviously incapable of recognizing a set-down even if bludgeoned with one. Keeping her own gloved hands firmly on her reticule, Thea said pleasantly, but with a seldom heard edge to her voice,

"I beg you will forgive me, but I do not collect to have met you at the Dillinghams', madam. Perhaps *your* name. . . ."

The woman bridled, but the man gave a genuine, if reluctant, bark of laughter and apologized, explaining that concern about their niece must explain and excuse their behavior. He then introduced himself as Sir Humphrey Barrett, George's uncle, and then presented Hannah, his wife. They seldom came to town and were here at present only reluctantly, for personal reasons.

It was impossible to find any fault with this, and Thea, feeling obscurely relieved that her young friend was, after all, with unexceptionable relatives, came down off her high ropes and was her normal, amiable self. But she could not like the Barretts and was relieved when, after a brief exchange of courtesies, they said they must leave. As she was about to part from them, however, she caught the anxious, even desperate, gleam in her young acquaintance's eyes and, changing her mind about her direction, said pleasantly to Lady Barrett,

"Ma'am, I was but now on my way to see Mrs. Dillingham's eldest daughter, Maria Lady Barton, who is visiting her mama briefly during the Season, although she seldom leaves her young daughter alone with her nurse in the country. Can I not prevail on you to let . . . George . . . accompany me? I assure you," she added hastily, seeing the dubious look on both faces, "I shall bring her back myself in my carriage. And as for walking now, why, they are only just around the corner in Berkeley Square."

There was a pause, while the Barretts presumably debated within themselves whether to let George go, and Thea thought what a farouche name for so fragile and feminine a young girl. At last Sir Humphrey said, in a manner far less urbane than his more recent conversation,

"Oh, very well. It can do no harm, I suppose. George, I expect to see you home at Upper Grosvenor Street within the hour—at most." And then, to Thea, with patent insincerity,

"Madam, your servant. I am obliged to you. Come, Hannah."

Thea, left standing on the pavement with a silent George, reflected that it would not have mattered to them had she been engaged for the entire day with the Dillinghams: Sir Humphrey had decreed that she bring George home within the hour and that—to his mind—was that. A moment's fury shook her, but then her sense of humor rose at the ridiculous position she had put herself in, and she began to laugh. George, who had perhaps seen the thunder on her new friend's brow, now began to smile too. Thea, noting the pretty brown eyes so relieved in the round young face, felt the last vestiges of her resentment vanish and said amiably,

"But your name *cannot* be George . . . what is it, my dear? Georgina, Georgiana?"

"Georgina—and I always used to be *called* so," came the reply in so forlorn a voice that Thea's heart melted.

"And—forgive me—your parents?"

"My father is . . . abroad. My mother died a little over two years ago."

Thea, whose own mother had died some ten years ago when she herself was about the same age as this young girl, felt a pang of pity. However, she sensed that any deep expression of sympathy might well upset the precarious calm of her new acquaintance.

"How *very* distressing for you. I lost my Mama when

I was about your age, and I was devoted to her. But, you know, one does recover from such a loss. Indeed, one must take pains to do so."

Feeling that any reference to Georgina's father, so hesitantly described as "abroad," might bring uncomfortable revelations from this strange girl with her odd relatives, she continued gently,

"Your mother would wish it, I am sure."

To this Georgina replied, with unexpected spirit, that her mother would also wish her to be called Georgina, and *enjoy* herself a little.

"She was always so pretty, you see, and wore lovely clothes, and, and . . . had such a busy life with parties, and balls . . ." Her lip trembled and she stopped abruptly.

Thea, somewhat at a loss and anxious not to appear to connive with the girl in what was an obvious criticism of her aunt and uncle, felt that she had perhaps so far taken a rather one-sided view of the situation. She said kindly,

"But I suspect you are not yet 'out,' and must wait a little for such excitements."

Georgina looked at her sadly and responded with a curious air of resignation,

"You are correct, ma'am, I should not come out until next Season. But it will not be, I am sure of it. Apart from anything else, I should be totally unprepared, quite *gauche*, you know. For I attend none of the classes—dancing, deportment, pianoforte, or harp, perhaps, that girls of my *present* age must, if they are to conduct themselves properly when they *do* come out. Still less am I allowed to learn anything . . . with my *mind*, you know."

Although she realized the necessity of such lessons as dancing and deportment, Thea privately held most young females who were considered "prepared" for their Season to be absolute ninnies. She was touched and interested to hear that Georgina also wished to use her *mind*. It seemed rather shabby of the Barretts, even if by chance they had no time for the frivolities of 'coming out,' to refuse to allow Georgina to take, say, French or Italian, or even drawing lessons. But perhaps they were in straitened circumstances—although she doubted this, considering the elegance of Lady Barrett, the sleek carriage and coachman glimpsed down the passageway, and the rich, if somber, attire of Sir Humphrey. Perhaps Georgina's father then was without a feather to fly with, or even in debt. That might account for the mysterious intonation of the word 'abroad' earlier in George's conversation. How little she knew of these people! And, she realized suddenly, how little she wished to know. She glanced down at Georgina again, to find the brown eyes studying her anxiously.

"Have I said something to offend you, ma'am?"

Thea laughed. "No, of course not! I was just wool-gathering!" She felt, however, constrained to add, "But perhaps you will tell me why you ran from the carriage in such a manner, my dear. It is hardly the thing, so you must have had some cogent reason."

Georgina flushed, and bit her lip. Her reply was faint.

"I . . . no. It is just, you see, that sometimes my aunt will not cease to berate me. I am stupid and a nuisance, I know, but to be continually told so! It suddenly becomes more than I can bear!"

Thea reflected privately that Hannah Barrett must be

a most unpleasant scold to drive a seemingly biddable and shy girl to the extreme of running from a vehicle in the open street, and that Georgina herself must be almost at the end of her tether. All she said, however, was that now Georgina had such friends as the Dillinghams and herself, she might feel less confined and less a nuisance to her aunt. Georgina received this statement with docility and no comment and was spared any further conversation on the subject as at that moment they reached the neat steps, the smart railings and the heavy imposing door of the Dillinghams' house.

They were received impeccably by Stukely, well known and liked by Thea since the days when she and Maria were always together, and on inquiring after Lady Barton and the youngest Dillingham girl, Lucy, who was Georgina's friend, were told that the entire female side of the family were assembled in the drawing room. This comprised no fewer than five girls, three of them married, and their very active mama, a widowed matriarch of large proportions.

"A family conference?" Thea asked Stukely, intending, if so, to take herself and her companion off at once, for she had all the small family's distrust of a large assembly of relations in private discussion.

"No, Miss, not at all. Just a chance gathering, really— Miss Maria down from Lancashire and staying with her mama, as you must know, and Miss Jane and Miss Amelia here in town with their husbands for the Season. And the other young ladies," he smiled kindly at Georgina, "still in the schoolroom, but here in London with their governess."

Thus reassured, Thea and Georgina allowed Stukely

to escort them up the wide, gracefully curved staircase
and into the salon to be welcomed effusively, if rather
overpoweringly, by the assembled Dillinghams. These
ladies were extremely handsome and elegant, but built
on such Junoesque lines that even Thea, who, though
very slender, was quite tall, seemed to dwindle considerably, while Georgina, petite in every way, was swamped.
But she noticed how Georgina blossomed in the warmth
of such affection. Her apprehensive manner quite vanished and, having made a warm but suitably correct
greeting to Mrs. Dillingham, she was soon chattering fast,
although not foolishly, to that lady's three younger daughters, including Amelia, who though married, was scarcely
out of the schoolroom herself. Thea, with Mrs. Dillingham, Maria, and Jane, was soon conversing less ob-
streperously, though just as contentedly. Not having met
for several days, they began composedly and with only a
little malice, to discuss the recent *on-dits* and fashions
of their elegant world.

Chapter 2

A_{LL} the Dillingham girls were good-natured as well as large, and once one became accustomed to their mother's authoritative manner, one found her, too, a very good sort of woman, sincerely anxious for everyone's happiness, even if a little too inclined to dictate what form that happiness should take. Perhaps this was the result of her husband's death when the youngest was but a year old, which left his wife with more than adequate means, but also with five daughters to bring up and out and marry off. Thea was fond of her and, with her own quick, sensitive mind, already realized that Mrs. Dillingham had hidden depths of dry humor and unconventionality within her.

She caught a glimpse of this now, as she explained lightly to her hostess that she and Georgina could not sit with them for long, as Sir Humphrey looked to see his niece back within the hour, and they must therefore soon continue on to Thea's house to command Mr. Langham's carriage for the longer journey back to Sir Humphrey's. A curious steely gleam appeared in Mrs. Dillingham's eye as she remarked, dryly, that with so much leisure each day as they all undoubtedly had, it must be stimulating to be forced to race, like the Royal Mail Coach, from place to place on a strict timesheet. Observing Georgina to be far away, seated in the big window embrasure with her young friends, she then continued in a low voice to Thea,

"I did not know you were familiar with Sir Humphrey and his . . . lady,"—again the steely flicker—"they are nearer your parents' generation than yours, my dear Thea, and have anyway been . . . out of circulation, shall we say? . . . for quite some years."

Thea, explaining briefly the circumstances of her morning meeting, could not resist asking about Georgina's father. Mrs. Dillingham smiled.

"He was the younger brother, a good many years junior to Humphrey, and far easier. But I cannot collect overmuch about him. They were always an odd family—good blood, you know, but definitely odd. Their estates—quite considerable, one understood—were in the north somewhere . . . Lancashire . . . Yorkshire? and as the boys' parents had a quite incomprehensible hatred of London, they seldom came up here."

At this point she was distracted by Maria, who had been working quietly at her embroidery but who now glanced up to say in an irrepressible, if low voice, "Mama, you will soon be discussing poor Georgina's gothic uncle and aunt again." And then, seeing the look of disapproval on her mother's face, added appeasingly, "Well, one can't exactly call them gothic, perhaps, but there's *something* grotesque about them, all the same!"

With this Thea was inclined to agree, but all further possibility of conversation on the matter was cut short by Lucy's running back to them with Georgina close behind her. She asked her mother, a little shyly, whether she might take her friend up to the schoolroom and show her the new book of aquatints of birds and flowers, which Mrs. Dillingham had recently bought her. Lucy, through her governess's excellent instruction, was quite knowledgeable about flora and fauna. Her mother agreed with an involuntary instruction to both girls to Walk, not Run, since they were now fast becoming young ladies.

"But remember, girls, no longer than ten minutes. That is all the time we are to be spared our visitors today!"

Thea noticed, if Mrs. Dillingham did not, the swift flush that stained poor Georgina's cheeks, and recognizing a quick, even oversensitive mind, smiled encouragingly in her direction. Her hostess watched the now sedately retreating backs of the two girls and said an absent-minded farewell to the newly wed Amelia, who was going to her milliner's, and to Selina, who still shared the schoolroom with Lucy, but loved to watch on such occasions.

"You would think, would you not, that even if the *uncle* is so careless of others' convenience, the *aunt* would not be so? A man can seem merely inconsiderate where, in similar circumstances, a woman is positively ill-bred. But although I do not know her well, I am certain that Hannah Barrett, my dear, is jumped up. I grant you she has an air, a certain elegance—she may even have a fortune of her own—but her *mind* is coarse!"

Thea, who did not agree with the distinction between behavior permissible in a man and in a woman, and who, (although she suspicioned Mrs. Dillingham's judgment to be correct), knew nothing of Lady Barrett, for once found herself at a loss for an answer. Her companion smiled a crocodile smile, and glanced sidewise at Maria, who was laughing, and at Jane, who looked bored.

"I do seem a little obsessed with two unpleasing acquaintances, do I not? The fact is, I was very much put out by them both the other day—and sorry for that poor child." She settled her ample bulk in her elegant chair, covered in gold and silver Indian chintz, and went on, speaking solely now to Thea,

"It was but a short while ago—my sister and her husband were giving a small birthday party for their youngest girl. She is already fifteen, you may collect, and one would have thought too old for such junketings, but the fact is that with all the rest of the family so much older, she has rather a thin time of it. So my brother-in-law, Haversham, who is a most indulgent father, hit on the idea of a simple gathering—not too childish, with perhaps some games like Fish or Beggar-my-Neighbor, and a little simple dancing among the girls. Lucy and Selina were, of course, invited, and quite a number of their friends, so that the only unknown among the company was this shy, rather dowdy, but quite pretty little female called Georgina."

At this point, Thea noticed a resigned look pass between Maria and Jane. But they remaining silent and attentive, Mrs. Dillingham continued,

"I was just about to ask my sister who she might be, when Haversham himself came up, to ask for Lucy and Selina's indulgence. As the friendliest and most popular of the girls, would they keep an eye on her? He explained that she was Miles Barrett's daughter, briefly in London, seldom seen, always kept very close, and living in the North with Miles's elder brother, Humphrey, and his wife. 'A quite impossible woman,' he called her."

Thea nodded and, remembering Georgina's plaint about her own social shortcomings, asked how she had seemed with the other young people. Mrs. Dillingham raised her eyes heavenward.

"Quite without any social accomplishments, although I will say, her behavior was good. Still, she could not dance, nor sing, nor even *attempt* the pianoforte. Really quite sad. Indeed, you know the way girls will chatter about bonnets and so on. Well, she seemed incapable of even that!"

She shook her head reflectively, then went on, in satisfied yet wholly pleasant tones,

"But the girls did look after her, Lucy particularly, and you could see how quickly she appreciated this. They even began to show her some dancing steps they had recently learned at Madam Mostyn's Academy of Dance, and I will say she heeded them very well, too."

Thea smiled. "So the friendship began!"

"Yes. Lucy especially quite took to her and wants to help her. Why, I shouldn't be surprised if they are not practicing more dancing steps or some such thing now, after a very cursory look at those aquatints!"

Mrs. Dillingham glanced down at her hands and spread them, a habit she had before making some arbitrary, or even cutting, statement.

"But the aunt and uncle! She is so ill-mannered! I must tell you later how she spoke to me at the time . . . and he is so offhand as to be boorish! Yet he *is* a gentleman, you know, albeit a rude one!"

This time Thea who, again contrary to the prevailing attitude of her time, believed that rudeness, deliberate or not, formed no part of a *gentleman's* make-up, held her tongue. Mrs. Dillingham was elderly, and anyway entitled to the opinions held by her world. Thea merely asked, therefore,

"They have no children of their own, then?"

"No, he married late in life. Unwisely, as is often the case. Not," she added hastily, "that I approve of a man's marrying too young. There is," she fixed her eye firmly on Thea, "a Happy Mean!"

Thea, rightly taking this as a reference to Amelia's husband, who was quite considerably older, contented herself this time with merely nodding. Mrs. Dillingham, caught between such a general observation and her present story, lost the thread of her discourse and was forced to ask her daughters,

"Maria, Jane, where was I?"

"With little Georgina at the Havershams', Mama," said Maria good-temperedly.

"Of course! I vow I get more addle-brained every day! I was about to tell you of Lady Barrett's behavior, was I not? It was nothing, really, I suppose, but so—graceless is the only word I can use; and so unkind to her niece. I was looking on at the little dancing lesson and thinking, I admit, how handsome my youngest two were, when the insufferable woman came bustling up to me and presumed, on a very short acquaintance this Season (for the Barretts are so seldom in Town I have not met her more than twice before in my life), to observe that she did not hold with such frivolous behavior in young girls, that chits are permitted to grow up too fast these days, and that undoubtedly many will end up with morals as light as their wits!"

Thea looked, and indeed felt, suitably shocked, and Mrs. Dillingham, nodding like a mandarin, held up her hand to show there was worse to come.

"Before I could give her a freezing set-down, she flounced away, saying they must, anyway, take Georgina home soon. It's my belief, you know, she misliked seeing the child either happy or even a little independent! Why, I hear she is forever whispering behind her hand, bewailing the absence of the child's father, and hinting how 'noble' her husband is to house his niece with, possibly, no hope of any return. Indeed, she has even been heard to complain how much Georgina is costing them!"

At this conversational turn, gossip though it might be, Thea could not resist asking if Mrs. Dillingham could not possibly remember more about Georgina's missing father, and Maria and Jane at once added their request to hers. Mrs. Dillingham (reflecting that her girls were already married, and Thea was almost too free of any missish delicacy) closed her eyes, concentrated for a minute or two, and then began slowly.

"He vanished. Yes, that was it! And something less

than two years ago, if I have the right of it. His wife died
a short while previously, and he had loved her so deeply
that he became perhaps a little unbalanced, anyway
quite . . . unrestrained . . . in his behavior, especially
where women were concerned. Of course, I collect hearing he had been a wild one before his marriage, but he
had settled down well into domestic happiness. One can
only suppose that when this was brutally cut short, his
grief and loneliness drove him to such excesses . . ."
She shook her head sadly, perhaps remembering her own
bereavement so many years ago or considering how many
responsibilities her tragic loss had laid on her. Thea had
a sudden astonishing vision of a younger but still stout
Mrs. Dillingham driven by grief to excesses with assorted
gentlemen instead of to a worthy and useful life bringing
up her daughters. Hysteria seemed very close, and heartily
tired of her unfortunate sense of humor, she said the first
thing that came into her head.

"But . . . how strange that I don't recall it! It must
have caused *some* stir! And," she added with a twinkle,
"as you are very well aware, ma'am, I have been out of
leading strings a very long time now!"

"Oh, it was kept very close. Besides, I collect you must
have been away in Scotland with your grandfather, my
dear. For you left the same time, did you not, as Maria
did for her honeymoon in Italy?" She alded flatly, cyni-
cally, as Thea concurred with this, "And all was forgotten by the time you returned, no doubt. The *on-dits*
thrust up and wither fast as mushrooms among the gossips,
do they not?"

This was undoubtedly true, yet Thea remained intrigued.

"But . . . he has *never* been seen since?"

"No. He did not return home from one of his secret . . . debauches or excursions or whatever. And none of his friends, whether suitable or unsuitable (and I may say he had many of both, for he was always *liked*), knew where he was. It was even taken up by the constables, I believe, for he was well known, too, and wealthy. But nothing came of it. The prevalent opinion was that he could have been accidentally killed in some brawl about one of his light-skirts; or in a duel, perhaps, though not here in England, for that would certainly have come to light . . . but no one knew."

"Poor little Georgina," said Thea, moved.

"Exactly so, my dear—although she was at least young enough, and secluded enough in more northern counties, for the full horror of the situation not to touch her. Think if she had been older and had already taken her place here in London!"

"She was living in the North, in the same establishment as her father, when all this happened, then?"

Uncertainty, then memories, chased each other across Mrs. Dillingham's broad face. "Well, she was frequently in the same house with him. Gossip said he took his pleasures locally and seldom came South, I recall, but . . . now . . . what was it? Ah, yes, I collect that the only firm information to come out of the matter was that Miles had approached his brother, Humphrey, the day previous to his disappearance and asked him to take Georgina, her maid, and her governess in 'for a day or so.' Though no explanation was given for the request."

"And Sir Humphrey agreed?" asked Thea, thinking he

could not be so harsh as he seemed if he had performed that one act of kindness.

"Yes. I believe he has *some* family feeling, or he would not have harbored Georgina so long. But it seems he took her in on the understanding that it was only for a *few* days, as his wife kept reiterating later. Neither of them had any time for children, and indeed, Humphrey was about to ride over to his brother's (their estates were not *too* far distant) to complain that he could keep Georgina no longer, when it was realized that Miles was in truth missing. And, naturally, even Humphrey had not the heart to send her away then. So she has remained with them, waiting with diminished hope for her father's return, ignored by her uncle, and patronized, even disliked, by her aunt, ever since."

Maria lifted her head from her embroidery, which she had resumed during her mother's conversation.

"Lady Barrett certainly resents her presence, Thea. It is obvious to the dullest intelligence. I am perhaps a little better acquainted with her than Mama, since William's eastern boundaries are not too far from Sir Humphrey's in one quarter, and as he and William share an interest in hunting and such like, you know. And the little I see of her, she is *never* kind, *never* easy!"

Here Maria cast a quick glance at her mother and then went on resolutely,

"People up there say she is a vulgar woman, and it is solely a matter of money with her. Miles Barrett is not *known* to be dead, his estates are carefully tied up, and poor Georgina can hope for nothing from these but her comparatively insignificant pin money. For naturally, Sir Humphrey will not wish to make claims for her and become involved with all the formalities attendant on a presumption of death—at least not at this stage. He has no need, for he is himself very wealthy. And, to be fair, it is said he is no skinflint with money, as his wife is. Still it comes to the same thing; for where *he* is merely impatient with the situation, which has dragged on unexpectedly from month to month, and now year to year, *she* is bitterly resentful, refusing to lay out even a penny more than she need, whether on clothes, or little luxuries, or social occasions for her niece. And as he is a hard man with no time for children or young girls, and not much imagination . . . well, I would say the poor girl's situation must be quite desperate!"

Mrs. Dillingham, who had been staring at her daughter with raised eyebrows, now said in considerable surprise,

"I had no notion, Maria, that you were so well informed!"

"Do you vastly disapprove, Mama?"

Mrs. Dillingham, looking suspiciously at her daughter's insincerely demure face, with laughter lurking just below the surface, hesitated, and then responded in an amused voice that yet held a sigh,

"No, my dear! But how quickly you are grown up! It seems but a little time since I should have had to take you to task for even listening to such vulgar gossip."

In the general laugh that followed, Lucy and Georgina arrived breathless, full of apologies for their lateness. But Mrs. Dillingham, who was fair as well as strict, remarked it did not signify, since their elders had forgotten the time too. She then insisted on ordering the carriage for Thea, since she and Georgina would not now have time to return on foot to Thea's own house in Charles

Street and order her carriage for the drive back to Sir Humphrey's, a good deal further distant in Upper Grosvenor Street.

"And as Sir Humphrey," said Mrs. Dillingham, with a wide, ambiguous stare, "must *not* be kept waiting, you must, of course, leave directly from here!"

Chapter 3

THEA'S encounter with Sir Humphrey on bringing Georgina home had been rather uncomfortable. They were admitted to a richly appointed house where the rather vulgar hand of Lady Barrett could be detected by Thea's discerning eye in the numbers of small tables, ormulu clocks, and draperies, and were received by Sir Humphrey and his wife in the withdrawing room with marked cold disapproval. Holding his timepiece in his hand, he stated without preamble and directly to George that they were well nigh ten minutes late. His wife rose with a flounce and added in a scold's voice and also to Georgina, that this was what came of allowing a girl out virtually on her own.

If Thea had not suddenly wondered with amusement whether every visitor to the house, or friend of the Barretts, were ignored, or addressed indirectly through

poor little Georgina, she would have replied with some
disapproval at once. As it was, while she wrestled again
with her sense of the ridiculous, the moment passed: Sir
Humphrey indicated a chair, and Lady Barrett, after
dismissing Georgina to her room to remove her pelisse,
asked, somewhat ungraciously, if Thea would like some
refreshment, such as ratafia or a glass of wine, perhaps.
This Thea refused with a coldness equal to their reception
of her, and would have left at once without ceremony,
had it not been that poor Georgina, so summarily dismissed to remove her outer garments, obviously looked
to say good-bye to her new friend. She therefore sat down
and addressed herself to passing the hopefully brief time
before Georgina's return as pleasantly as possible, by
remarking, not on the latest dazzling and exorbitant
banquet given by the Regent, (which she herself markedly
disapproved of as a sinful waste of the nation's money),
but on the situation in the North and the Midlands where
the Luddites had again been at work smashing machines.
She had chosen this topic with the best of intentions as a
good talking point: Lady Barrett was said to disapprove
of frivolity in the young at least, and so presumably in the
middle-aged too; both the Barretts were said to dislike
London and its Society; and finally, Sir Humphrey's
estates were no great distance from those regions where
industrial unrest had been two years ago, and indeed still
was, a constant thorn in the side of the government.

But Lady Barrett merely gave her a wide stare of
incomprehension, and Sir Humphrey raised fierce blue
eyes, under bristly brows, to her face and said briefly,

"Should be hanged, all of them. Magistrates far too

lenient! Can't stand in the way of progress. Country's going soft."

Thea was too bookish. She knew it. But she was also too impulsive, and where she felt deeply could, or rather would, never hold her tongue. She now raised equally fierce though far more attractive eyes to Sir Humphrey and answered coolly that if *he* were a simple weaver, perhaps working from home, and saw his master fitting a machine in a new factory that would do the work of six men, *he* might be tempted to destroy the monster loom. Or worse, if he saw shoddy work being produced on a wider, but inferior, stocking loom, as in Nottinghamshire, he might almost be said to be morally correct in rejecting the latter. Though, of course, his *methods* could only be called reprehensible. And the same mitigating circumstances applied, in her opinion, to the agricultural workers too.

The thought that he might be a weaver, or a farm hand, or any sort of workman, had so obviously never entered Sir Humphrey's head that his body went practically rigid with surprise. On top of this, the fact that so attractive a creature should be so familiar with the problems posed by the Luddites suddenly struck him almost like a blow. The result, to Thea's wicked eye, was ludicrous, so that Lady Barrett had the experience of watching both her companions struggling with two very different emotions. It was Thea who recovered first, saying prettily that Sir Humphrey must forgive her, she was, she knew, too interested in matters that should not concern her. Sir Humphrey, seeing no sarcasm, as she knew he would not, in this remark, waved his hand placatingly and added—

more mildly than she had expected—that for his part, being a man of the land himself, he had no time for these newfangled *industrial* high larks. But that all such machines would increase, and the factories and mills to house them also—and there was not a damned thing anyone could do about it.

"As for threshing machines and such like, well, I think we, as landowners, have a duty to protect those who work manually on the land. But get most of the farmers to see matters in that light!" He threw up his hands, and the corners of his mouth turned down.

Thea looked at him gravely. So gravely indeed that he added, surprised at himself for talking so to a woman,

"The factories wouldn't be too bad, you know, if the owners all looked after their men, housed them as we do our farm workers—well, some of us anyway—and kept things in repair generally. And saw their factory hands didn't want if they got sick or too old for work." He added suddenly, "Of course, Jacobins and Paineites are behind a lot of the trouble-making, not the craftsmen themselves or the laborers, these days. It's the devil!"

He then continued, seemingly on a tangent, "I suppose you have never visited a factory, Miss Langham?" When she admitted never having done so, he went on, "They are not too bad, the few I have remarked. Light and spacious —lots of windows, you know. And some—but only a very few, I think—have just such little cottages as I mention alongside them."

Thea was agreeing at this point that such a kind of paternalism was no bad thing when Lady Barrett broke in, obviously having pursued her own train of thought, to say that Sir Humphrey was considered an excellent landlord, all his cottages were thatched and repaired, and his people generally satisfied.

In spite of herself, Thea could not keep the initial surprise from her face, both at Lady Barrett's sudden pride in her husband's reputation, and perhaps at that reputation itself. To her chagrin, she had been observed.

"Surprised you, haven't I?" Sir Humphrey grinned rather wolfishly. "Saw no good in me, did you, young lady?"

Addressed as young lady and her opinion diagnosed so exactly, Thea could not but laugh. She answered him warmly.

"I must apologize. My friends tell me I sometimes make too hasty judgments. I must guard against it. But all the same, I should like to know why you wish to hang the Luddites, sir. Especially in view of your later, shall we say, more temperate, even kindly, thinking!"

"They must be put down, or they will be used," Sir Humphrey said flatly, "both by this damned reactionary government, to stop any kind of reform, and by evil revolutionaries to further their own far more dangerous ends. Mark my words, the Luddites will be used as—as bogey men. To frighten good folk in their beds, and make the excuse for even harsher laws and taxes. And at the same time the republicans will work under their cover!" Here he glanced at Thea to see if he still had her attention (his wife's thoughts were seemingly wandering) and, satisfied with her continued interest, went on,

"I speak now not of agriculture which I feel sure will come to terms with itself in time, but of industry: if these hotheads would just wait a little or talk to their owners, a lot of them, I am sure, would be amenable to fair dealing. Why, many owners started from just such humble stations in life themselves!"

"And are consequently uncouth, unreasonable, and ruthless!" interjected Lady Barrett unexpectedly. It crossed Thea's mind that perhaps this was where Hannah Barrett's money had come from—and her spurious good manners: a ruthless, harsh, hated father.

Sir Humphrey regarded his wife sardonically,

"Uncouth, possibly. Ruthless? Well, I don't know. Anyway, less ruthless and more sensible than this government. At least they realize it's not to their advantage to have what almost amounts to civil war on their hands . . . I am a Whig," he added, drawing himself up.

"No one would have imagined it!" murmured the irrepressible Thea. But this time her lighthearted sarcasm was recognized, and Sir Humphrey was about to reply when Georgina came back into the room, her hair smoothed, her eyes downcast, and a general air of apprehension so apparent that Thea's new feeling of friendship for Sir Humphrey and tolerance for his wife vanished. She rose at once, saying she must go, then smiling gently at poor Georgina, added deliberately,

"You must come and visit me next time, instead of our going to the Dillinghams'. If your aunt and uncle will allow it, of course."

She waited not at all for any reply to this, preferring rather to let the suggestion settle and be talked out, perhaps even argued between Sir Humphrey and his spouse. Hastily she said her farewells to the Barretts and was soon seated once more in the carriage returning home at a far more leisurely pace than she had come.

She was annoyed to find therefore that her next encounter with Sir Humphrey took place but a few days later. Thea and her father (who did not find themselves too often in the same company) were on this occasion engaged to dine with an old friend of Mr. Langham's, who was also Thea's godfather. They had but seated themselves, and started to converse with guests who had already arrived, when Sir Humphrey and Lady Barrett were announced.

Thea's father looked up with some amusement (for his daughter had given him a witty account of the couple, as well as a more serious description of Sir Humphrey's dissertation on domestic politics). Thea's face registered exasperation. But there was no hope for it; even less at dinner, where Thea found herself placed on Sir Humphrey's right after a brief, discreet apology and explanation from her host that Sir Humphrey was unused to town, had no small talk to charm the fair sex, and that only someone as astute and as pretty as Thea could be expected to cope with him.

They struggled along until the covers were removed with pigeons and asparagus, when Sir Humphrey said, suddenly irritable,

"No good mincing on like this, Miss Langham! Let us talk of something sensible, if you please. Something," he added in explanation of what even he must have felt to be some rudeness, "worth speaking of."

Thea turned her fine eyes towards him and asked, with a wicked glint in them,

"Well, sir, what shall it be? The Prince's latest tiff with his outlandish wife? Or his magnificent banquets? Or the latest scandal about Lady Caroline Lamb?"

He looked amused, but growled at her very low, "Exactly what I mean. No one speaks of anything worthwhile. Well, I make no bones about it, I hate it down here. I expect you've been told. Everyone frantically enjoying himself so as to avoid the boredom. Those damn silly dandies, Alvaney and such, gaming on flies crawling up the windows, or taking hours to fit a coat, or arrange a new fall for a cravat. Or witless females gossiping, and reading rubbishy novels, or intriguing, or fainting, or going to the milliner's. My God! The men would be better off tending their estates instead of stripping them; and the women could at least see to the furniture and linen and such being well kept, even if they can't stop the fortunes and houses falling apart!"

Thea recognized there was some truth in this outburst, but said all the same, very mildly,

"But everyone isn't so, you know, Sir Humphrey! My father likes the Season still, despite his years of widowhood, yet he is an excellent landlord. And again, at this very dinner, Lord Stokes and the exquisite dandy across from him are also conscientious landowners, as well as being very wealthy!"

He looked at her, laughed briefly, and spoke without malice.

"You don't like extreme statements; or, indeed, extremes of any sort, do you, Miss Langham?"

"No. I believe in moderation in everything."

"Ah, then you're a Whig like me!"

"No!" she said sharply this time. "I am neither Whig nor Tory. I am . . . myself."

"Ah, Thea. A Goddess! A law to herself!"

It was now her turn to laugh briefly, but the remark, in its similarity to that of her cousin, brought an image of that impudent young man again to her mind. And from that memory it was no effort to recall that it was of him she had been thinking when Georgina had fallen against her in Bruton Street. She asked slowly,

"How is Georgina?"

"Well, I thank you."

"Is she . . . will she . . . be taking the dancing lessons she so hankers for?"

Sir Humphrey's stare made it obvious that he felt this to be no concern of Thea's, but that since she was so obviously an eccentric he would deign to answer her. He said briefly,

"I fear not. We return North soon, you know, and as we lead a very quiet life there, she will have no need of them."

"You and your wife don't approve of such frivolities?"

He gave her another stare. "I cannot answer for my wife. For myself, no, I do not. Not on moral grounds, you understand. Merely that they are a waste of a woman's time, which could be better employed in other ways."

It was Thea's turn to stare. "You feel the same about worthier matters too? Music, the arts, languages and so on, where women are concerned?"

He looked at her sidewise, obviously mistrusting the mildness of her voice. And then utterly disarmed her by saying, in a conciliatory fashion,

"Look, Miss Langham, don't bait me! Providing she's good-looking, I like an accomplished, intelligent woman as well as anyone. Better than some, I might say. But Georgina! She has no . . . no *style*. Start teaching her French or Italian or music even, and she'd be a *bas bleu* in no time. I mean, she's mousy already in her manner and looks; add a little learning. . . !" He threw up his hands in horror, and Thea, by now justifiably angry, could not resist pointing out that Georgina's lack of poise, of address, her general mousiness—as he would doubtlessly put it—were in good part due to the grievous gap in her social education which she felt sorely. Given the proper social upbringing, her air, her manner, her looks, all would improve; and at least a little culture would then enhance her personality without the risk of being dubbed, so cruelly, a bluestocking.

Sir Humphrey, however, remained unconvinced and it was with relief that Thea was claimed in conversation by the gentleman on her left.

Chapter 4

IT was the first night of the great Fireworks Display which the Prince Regent had ordered to be set up in Green Park. Although the Season was virtually over, everyone was going, from the richest and most fashionable to the poorest, for there were said to be, among other delights, the greatest display of rockets ever seen. A tremendous finale, the Castle of Discord, at least a hundred feet high "with all its horrors of fire and destruction," would finally disappear in smoke to be replaced by the delicate tracery of a Temple of Concord.

The country, despite internal unrest and the terrible poverty among the lower classes, had been entertaining lavishly. First, there was the fat Louis XVIII, then the Csar of All the Russias and King Frederick of Prussia. Now, finally, to celebrate both Wellington and the Peace, the general populace were to be given a treat of fireworks in Green Park, as well as other delights, balloon ascents, temples, towers, and booths in other London parks, including a mock navy battle on the Serpentine. Many sensible folk were asking themselves what good all these Royal Visits and Entertainments would do the poor and the starving. Intermittently, the Prince himself had been booed by the populace. But such was Prinny's flair for effect and bonhomie, coupled with his truly good nature and his charm when he chose to exercise it, that on most such occasions, his gross extravagances were forgotten, and everyone entered into the spirit of whatever junketing was on hand.

Thea was feeling rather hagged, having dutifully attended endless receptions, banquets, and balls as well as arranging a few smaller, far more select parties of her own. But she felt she must nevertheless take in the fireworks also, as she had promised Georgina and several of her own young cousins that she would go with them and must be sure the party was suitably chaperoned. This, in fact, was quite difficult, for the young people were mostly only fifteen or sixteen, and full of such high spirits that they needed constant looking after in such a mixed assembly. In the end, besides herself, whom the world, if not Thea, would consider equally in need of chaperoning, she had succeeded in cajoling her witty young cousin of twenty, and a very stable friend of his, as well as two kindly and hopeless beaux of her own, to form the men of the group.

This evening then the party, having left their carriages, were all assembled in, as her cousin put it, a formation as tight and regimented as The Brigade, enjoying the Opening Display of Fireworks. But gradually, as the oohs and ahs increased, everyone relaxed a little; and, observing that they were completely surrounded by people very similar to themselves, (attempts had naturally been made by the authorities to create some kind of enclosures, and the strange tents set up haphazardly for cheap drink, food and all manner of trinkets, were some way distant and in Hyde Park), Thea's attention to her young flock wavered a little. She told herself that the escorts were keenly on the lookout for sneak thieves, pickpockets and the like, who might worm their silent, sinister way among the groups of spectators; the youngsters had been warned time and again not to stray; and she was being foolish to feel so tensed up.

Curiously enough, it was then as she relaxed, that she felt herself being watched. She turned her head to look around her, but it was difficult in the sharp flashes and sudden flickers of the fireworks to discern anyone clearly for any length of time. Faces were illuminated starkly, dead white, curiously fixed, for a second and then vanished again as if covered by a black blanket. Telling herself, with a little shake that she really was so fagged as to be becoming unhinged, Thea gave her attention once more (after privately counting her charges) to the Display, only to feel again this curious *concentration,* as it were, on her. More canny this time, she turned swiftly and succeeded to see a tall figure step backward, his head averted seemingly from the sudden glare; but when she glanced back again at the next illumination, no such tall figure was visible.

At this point the younger of her two admirers suggested that to see the set-piece better, they should move forward a little toward a slight rise in the ground. In this way, he insisted, they would be able to admire the whole wonderful machine. Accordingly, in a kind of phalanx, the party moved forward, with many military instructions and orders by the irrepressible young cousin, and some giggling by the young ladies of the party. Thea, moving with the rest, still not easy in her mind, glanced round again, swiftly and, she hoped, unobtrusively—and again caught a swift movement of withdrawal. She was now definitely nervous in spite of herself. She was used to being stared at, usually with admiration, but there was a furtive air about this occasion that made her uneasy. Open glances of approval, shy stares from timid, would-be admirers were one thing; but this sensation of being—the expression occurred to her suddenly—*stalked* was new to her. She therefore made a quick decision, for nervous though she might be, she did not lack courage and put her hand on the arm of her nearest escort, fortunately her cousin, and said firmly,

"I have seen a friend close behind us. I shan't get lost and will return within two minutes."

Her cousin, accustomed from his youngest days to being dominated by this fascinating elder relative, lost his opportunity to protest in the fractional pause caused by his wondering whether he should. In that second, between flashes, Thea was gone. She had slipped away under cover of the dark in roughly the direction where she had seen her supposed pursuer, and in the next livid flash found herself alongside although partly to the rear of him. Grasping her reticule firmly—it contained little for prudence's sake tonight, but had a heavy clasp which would swing well and heavily if necessary—she said clearly and without preamble,

"Why are you following our party?"

The tall figure, who had naturally been looking forward, gave a gasp of surprise, turned a startled, dark, and somewhat angry gaze full on Thea's face, bright momentarily in yet another revealing flash, and then said, in the unexceptionable tones of a gentleman,

"I was not aware, ma'am, that . . . that I was observed!"

Thea, who had been expecting the sentence to end with the statement that the stranger was not aware that he had been following them, felt the wind taken out of her sails a little. But she rallied and repeated severely,

"*Why* are you following us?"

There was a pause and during a series of now flickering flashes she had the opportunity to observe intermittently a thin, handsome countenance, with a long jaw, high-ridged nose, dark heavy eyebrows, and, surprisingly, a curved, almost too sensitive mouth. The color of his rather hooded eyes was indistinguishable in the uncertain light. The stranger, who had been observing her as closely as she him, now said slowly,

"I am certain I have the honor of addressing Miss Thea Langham . . . I . . . I . . . well, I am Miles Barrett."

If he had said he was Napoleon Bonaparte returned from Elba, or the Man in the Moon, Thea could not have been more surprised or overset. She remarked swiftly,

"But you're . . . everyone knows you to be . . ."

"Dead?" he asked sardonically. And Thea, feeling somehow set down, answered coldly,

"No. Missing. Perhaps sick or, possibly, dead." And then with her father's determination to pursue the main issue, "But you still have not explained what I can only call, sir, your furtive behavior tonight. Or how you come to know my name."

She added tersely, "Quickly, your answer, please. That is, if you want to preserve your strange privacy. My cousin will come searching for me soon."

He replied at once, with an air of assurance that she felt, in the circumstances, to be inexcusable,

"I wanted to study Georgina. Unobserved. I saw Humphrey this evening, immediately I arrived in town, and he told me of your destination . . . and a little of yourself . . ."

"Well, to be sure, having come to look for us and having had the amazing good fortune to find us in the crush, why did you not join us? *After* studying your daughter."

For the first time the stranger appeared a little discomposed. "I have only tonight discovered something of Georgina's life with the Barretts. I gleaned this unwittingly on their part. I never liked Hannah. And," he added bleakly, but so low that Thea could hardly hear him, "I had not realized my daughter would be so *grown*. I still think of her as she was when I left, just a child. And so, quite happy with them . . . which is certainly not the case!"

Exasperated, Thea observed that men were all alike, hopelessly self-centered, and so occupied with their own affairs as not to realize the world did not stand still for others although it must seem to for *them*. She finished gently, however, concerned by a curious bleakness glimpsed on his countenance,

"But you will meet her, won't you? I will even bring

her back to you now, if you wish it. I feel certain she will be overjoyed. Or if you think . . . well, perhaps tomorrow would be more . . . suitable . . ."

He interrupted in a voice in which cynicism and anguish were strangely mingled. "My dear Miss Langham, I am not at all certain that I should meet her at all . . . my life these past years . . . you do not know."

And then, as Thea looked at him with dawning comprehension and some pity, he asked urgently, yet still with that instinctive air of command,

"May I call on you tomorrow? But privately? From the little I have heard, I suspect you have been more than kind to Georgina. And I should value your advice concerning her."

The urgent appeal in his voice, underlined by the tense anxiety in the strong face revealed in the flickering light, overbore Thea's common sense and perhaps her propriety. She said quickly,

"At noon then, at my father's house in Charles Street." Walking hurriedly forward, she was just in time to prevent Miles Barrett's discovery by her cousin and a very angry elder beau who had come to search for her. It had been foolish, the latter said, to leave the line of carriages at all, merely because the young people were wishful to approach nearer the Display Site, and they must now make their way back to their vehicles at once. Thea, he knew, was always headstrong, but in this at least she should, and must, obey him.

Thea, who was aware his anger sprang only from concern for her, apologized meekly and affectionately. Relieved to be putting further distance between her party and Miles Barrett, she allowed herself to be ushered to where the carriages, coachmen, and two liveried servants were awaiting them.

Both Thea and her father were unfashionably early risers—he from prejudice and she, perhaps from his early disapproval, having little time for the current habit of lying abed until noon or later. It was about ten o'clock therefore that she was seated with Mr. Langham in his study next morning discussing some domestic financial detail, when she broke off to say rather apprehensively,

"I have a visitor coming this morning, sir, and to be frank with you, I am a little nervous, being quite unprepared how to deal with the matter."

"Some beau getting out of hand?" her father asked with a twinkle. "Or are you on the verge of finally deciding to give up running, and submit to married bliss at last?" Though a fond father, he was neither jealous or possessive, and added that if so, he hoped the fellow was worthy of her, and that he would immediately give his blessing, when something in her face stopped him.

"What is it, Thea?" he asked sharply. "Or rather, *who* is it?"

"Miles Barrett," she answered flatly and without preamble.

"*Miles* Barrett? But . . . let me think . . . surely he is . . ."

"Missing, or dead?" She gave a mirthless, reminiscent smile which was not lost on her father. "No, he's here in London. One might almost say skulking in London, for although he has seen his brother and sister-in-law, he seems anxious to meet no one else, not even his daughter."

Mr. Langham glanced narrowly at Thea. "And so, how did you come to meet him, Miss?"

"He was following our party at the Fireworks, he thought unobserved."

"You mean to tell me you left the carriages? And walked *afoot* last night?"

Ignoring the exasperation in her father's voice, Thea replied evenly, "Yes, Father. And it was all my doing. I thought it would be far more enjoyable for the young ones. And I collect I am always too headstrong, so you must not blame our escorts. The point I wish to make now, is that I was the only one to observe Miles Barrett. So naturally, when I could contrive it, I asked him privately what he wanted with us. I did not know then," she added hastily, seeing the thunder on her normally placid parent's brow, "who he was, of course!"

As Mr. Langham appeared momentarily bereft of words, she hurried on, anxious to avoid what she considered to be controversy irrelevant to the matter in hand.

"He said he had wished to see Georgina. Not to speak with her, for he feared his recent mode of existence might prevent his decently doing so . . . at least," she added, thinking back, "that is what I took him to mean. He was not explicit. But it is about this matter of Georgina that he wishes to ask my advice, I think, this morning. He had heard—or I should rather say, *concluded*—that I had befriended Georgina recently, you see. From Sir Humphrey and his wife. Concluded from them, I mean," she added in a small voice, for it was obvious her father was by now very angry indeed.

She sat meekly through a stern lecture on social behavior until finally, Mr. Langham, never a choleric man, ran out of steam like the northern Puffing Billy. She then pointed out gently that it was he himself who had taught her that women should be at least partly emancipated from an oversevere social code of appearances, and should rather follow the dictates of their natural good sense, dignity, and kindness, so as to steer a course between the tendentious puritanism of the Hannah Mores of this world, and the equally extreme gross libertinism of the Caroline Lambs; so he would surely agree, she concluded, that there was little else she could do in the circumstances except see Miles Barrett.

"He was altogether unexceptionable in his behavior, Papa; and conscience-stricken about Georgina. He had not thought to find her so grown, you see. It was quite sad. Indeed, I do feel that for poor Georgina's sake alone, I should see him."

She added with a smile, "No exception can be taken to my seeing him here within the house, my dear. And he but seeks my advice. I am sure he has no thoughts to outrage my feelings by tales of the past, or recent profligacy. If, indeed, they could be outraged, considering such wide reading as I have had!"

They both laughed at this, and Thea took the opportunity to add coaxingly,

"Come, Papa, I am no giddy miss, but a respectable lady of nigh on twenty-seven, who has run your home competently for you for many years. And I am convinced that, however much it may not *seem* the thing, it would not be kindly done to ignore Miles Barrett's request. You may rest assured that I shall not embroil myself in anything unseemly. And I promise," she finished, laughing outright now, "that I shall come scurrying to you for help if I find myself in any way at a standstill."

Mr. Langham did not laugh but smiled at least and finished the discussion by saying firmly,

"I shall remain at home this morning then. In the library. White's must do without my company." And Thea found nothing could move him from this decision.

At precisely noon a smart but unobtrusive carriage rolled to a stop outside the Langhams' house in Charles Street. Miles Barrett descended quickly and equally unobtrusively to raise the heavy knocker on the front door.

Thea, waiting a little apprehensively in the drawing room, heard Creevey's heavy tread as he marched to open the door and, having already been instructed by her to do so, immediately ushered the visitor, in dignified fashion, into the presence of the mistress of the house.

For his part, Miles Barrett, coming forward with tall elegance to make his bow, found himself unexpectedly impressed by the woman who turned to acknowledge him. His previous sight of her, in the half-dark between the vivid flashes of the Fireworks Display, although pleasing, had not prepared him for the grace, the slender charm, above all, the freshness of the girl before him. Her morning gown of green striped sarcenet, with its discreet flounces in the very latest fashion, its long sleeves, and its modest ruff, set off to perfection the copper highlights in the luxuriant curly hair. But above all the gentleness of countenance and the serenity in the fine hazel eyes lifted unsmiling to his affected his jaded spirits quite sharply. It was many years since he had had to do with fashionable, accredited beauties, and his chief memory of them was a kind of frenetic appeal far removed from the composure of the girl before him. Only his wife, he thought, with a terrible, sharp pang, had had a similar calm beauty. And poor Annabel too, of course, but in a different way.

With this reflection, however, the reason for his visit and the possible impropriety of his action in requesting it were recalled forcibly to his mind so that he said with considerably less address than usual,

"Miss Langham, I have been thinking . . . that is to say, it has been troubling me since we parted so hurriedly last night . . . that my request for your advice about Georgina must undoubtedly be an embarrassment to you . . . indeed that I have, as a stranger, asked altogether too much of you!"

The steady, beautiful eyes set in thick, dark lashes, considered him gravely, but he thought to glimpse the suspicion of a smile in them as Thea replied imperturbably,

"The same reflection did occur to my father this morning, sir, when I told him of our encounter. But he is an unusual parent, extremely fair-minded as well as kind and protective. And I persuaded him that, for Georgina's sake at least, I should see you."

She added, with a sudden obvious flash of amusement, "I have, anyway, long been in the habit of forming my own opinions and making my own decisions, you see. And I would not take such an undertaking—to discuss your daughter with you—lightly."

Miles Barrett, somewhat at a stand with surprise at this forthright self-analysis, murmured that he did not doubt it, and Thea continued,

"All the same, I cannot think what help or advice I could possibily give you without presumption, or indelicacy even, on my part."

She then sat down calmly and, indicating that her companion should do likewise opposite her, finished in an open friendly manner,

"Still, we both, I feel sure, have Georgina's interests, nay—happiness—at heart. And that surely is enough, is it not, to start with?"

During the expectant pause that followed, Miles found himself at a loss how to proceed, a state of affairs unusual for him. Inevitably, some of his reasons must be given for doubting the wisdom of being reunited with Georgina, however desirous he might be for such a reunion. Otherwise, what was the point in his being here to seek advice about his young daughter at all? He should, he thought almost distractedly, have chosen one of his older, experienced female friends as his confidante and mentor. Yet he had lost touch with them. And for all her comparative youth, Thea had not seemed last night (and did not now strike him) as lacking in experience or balance. Indeed, it was this combination of youthful openness and warmth with a strange, steady awareness— almost worldliness—as well as her obvious affection for Georgina, that had caused him impulsively to ask her advice in the first place. He sighed. He had always been too rash in his decisions, too hasty in his actions. He said slowly, in his deep voice,

"You must be aware that I now begin to realize where my impetuosity of yesterday has led me. It will not do to speak to you of my life this last year or so, and yet it is precisely because of this life that I need your advice about

. . . reintroducing myself to my daughter." He observed dryly, "I think, without conceit, that I may lay claim to a fairly extensive knowledge of your sex; but daughters are in a different category. And I have, quite literally, no conception of a growing daughter's susceptibilities, nor her sense of values, regarding a father!"

Thea did not immediately reply and, looking into the thoughtful eyes across from his, he added suddenly, "You are thinking, perhaps, I have made no attempt for a very long time to find out. Well, you are right. My only excuse, and a weak one, is that matters originally fell out in a certain way, and I acted then, and continued to act, impetuously, without due thought to every side of the question . . . whereas you, I feel sure, go about your affairs, whatever they may be, with consideration and forethought."

This, however, was more than Thea could support.

"Indeed, no! I am forever being taken to task for just such ill-considered impetuosity as you lay claim to. So I beg you to expect no censure on that score, at least!"

She laughed, but continued more seriously, "Also, I . . . I have had a rather unusual upbringing in that my mother having died young, I have been to a great extent under my father's aegis educationally. And he has the sensible notion that women's minds and feelings are as strongly superior as men's, so that they are as entitled as men to read anything, everything, that comes to hand, provided matter and manner are worthy, of course."

She finished with a smile. "I cannot, of course, claim to have firsthand knowledge of matters thought to be indelicate for female minds and ears. But I feel sure that the breadth of my reading, both ancient and modern, literary and scurrilous political, would surprise you. So I am not easily shocked. I say this, you see, so that you may feel able to speak freely where your . . . behavior . . . concerns Georgina." She concluded, devastatingly, "And let us, at least, be honest and admit that a great deal of this supposed delicacy is a sham: our Society is brutish beneath its elegant facade. It follows then that our minds are too."

Miles considered the speaker thoughtfully. Intelligence and an undoubted sense of humor, a keen eye and a wide, if sometimes bookish, experience of life, acquired by years of social awareness and omnivorous reading, had undoubtedly produced that very real air of sophisticated knowledge which he had originally detected interwoven with her normal poise and charm. For the first time, the dark features warmed into a real smile, and he said gratefully,

"Well, I must admit to a vast relief to hear you speak so. Briefly, then, my wife Jane died over two years ago, and as I had come to love her and to depend on her utterly, I was for a time literally beside myself. I tried to blot out my loss by returning to the, shall we say, rather ramshackle pastimes I had indulged in before my marriage. But after her gentle mind, her grace and beauty, I found these no panacea, but rather poison to me. So I decided, quite suddenly, to tour abroad again. In France a little . . . not for long, you know, as these things go."

He glanced at her briefly, rose, walked with his long stride toward the window through which a soft summery sky with fluffy, scudding clouds could be seen, and then returned to sit down abruptly again.

"I left Georgina with my brother, gave no indication

I was traveling abroad, and left. But I had hardly set foot in Paris when I literally ran into an old friend of mine who told me a—horrible story—about a little Parisian cyprian I had had a great deal to do with before my marriage." He raised his eyes fully to Thea's unwavering ones, and she realized with a sudden shock how intensely blue his were. "Annabel wasn't the usual run of mistresses. Her family had suffered during the Terror and she'd come down in the world, one might say. She had had very few lovers, I understood, and when I was there, well, there was *only* me . . ."

He added earnestly, "She was a . . . a nice little thing. Not a light-skirt. Someone you could talk to—and amusing, too. I was . . . very fond of her . . ."

He got up impatiently again, and having taken several agitated steps about the room, flung out his hands in a curious gesture, saying dismissively,

"Oh, God, what do the whys and wherefores matter now? The fact is, she was dying slowly of stomach cramps in awful poverty—which I could not understand, as I had left her well provided for, but no matter—and so I went to help her. I got her out of her sordid surroundings into a reasonable villa. And I stayed, discreetly, as she asked me, avoiding any contact with my friends, till the end."

He added, so low as to be almost unheard,

"She took far longer dying than the doctors I summoned to attend her expected. But by the time I came to realize this, gradually, it was too late to send messages to Humphrey. And I could not break my word and desert her. You may collect," he went on more firmly, staring hard at Thea, "that I had not told my brother where I was going in the first place. I wanted no contact with my previous life, and I planned to be away only a few weeks anyway. Then, afterward, I naturally did not tell him of my discovery of Annabel with all the embarrassment that would entail: I feel sure you have seen enough of Hannah and Humphrey to condone my silence on *this* point, especially. And, too, I imagined her end would be far swifter. And so I carried on from month to month; and with each successive month, it became more difficult to send any possible messages to England." There was a long silence until Thea said faintly,

"But . . . did you not think of Georgina? Could you not have sent word saying at least you were alive and well?"

"Of course, I thought of Georgina! But as a *child* still, young and easily amused, untroubled by fears for me. Not grown into a young woman and eating her heart out for news of me; or even for a little gaiety in a drab existence. You know Hannah, I understand. Well, Humphrey cannot keep his own counsel where she is concerned. Can you imagine, Miss Langham, the coil we should all have been in if I had declared the real situation to Humphrey even under supposed secrecy? Or, if I had merely said I was well but given no address? The turmoil, the questions, the *searches?* Come now, just think of it!"

Thea did and shuddered. She also, because she did not lack for imagination and therefore sympathy, could understand that Miles's distress for his little mistress, mingled with his bitter sense of loss of his beloved wife, could affect his judgment. She therefore merely said, gently,

"I can indeed understand how confused and tormented your thoughts must have been. And now you are wondering what reason you can give for your absence, sufficient to restore Georgina's confidence in you. I am sure her *affection* remains constant. But speculative tongues must be kept from wagging and causing her further distress."

At this, Miles Barrett gave her a strange look and said bluntly, "Exactly so."

"You have so far given no explanation to Sir Humphrey?"

"No. I suppose now I can botch some story up . . . prison for duelling, or a horrendous gambling debt perhaps . . . which, if he had heard of either during my absence, would have sent him hurrying to seek me out and redeem in one blow both myself and the family's honor—a state of affairs I would not stomach, as he would know." He added bleakly,

"But whatever story I tell will, it seems to me, of necessity have to be disreputable. And in the hands of that awful woman, Hannah, will be made to seem more so to upset Georgina." He stared broodingly at his clenched hands, his blue eyes seeing nothing of the elegance surrounding him. Then he said, seemingly on a tangent,

"Have you ever visited a slum, Miss Langham? A real slum, I mean—not a picturesque if overcrowded cottage, or some such, in the countryside."

Thea was strangely reminded of his brother's query regarding a factory, but before she had a chance to reply, Miles answered himself, his lip curling. "No, of course not. What do elegant women like you have to do with such things? Why should you spoil your pretty gowns, or your peace of mind, contemplating these horrors? You are not meant for such distress, but to grace our houses, our tables, our ballrooms with your fascinating presence!"

The criticism was not meant kindly. And Thea, who had often, in fact, felt great turmoil of mind contemplating the stunted children sometimes seen from her carriage windows, studying reports on the state of the agricultural poor, or, worse, on the starving new industrial areas in Lancashire and Yorkshire, flew up into the boughs, as her cousin would say, at once. She replied, equally bitterly,

"And what do *you* know of me, or women like me, Mr. Barrett? Why should you assume we are all empty-headed, unseeing, heartless, set only on pleasure? Or that we make no attempt to help others less fortunate than ourselves?"

"Aye! Like taking eggs from the home farm, or broth, to families on your father's estates perhaps. Or, if you are *very* brave and bold, visiting the poor when they are sick and perhaps even dangerously infectious!"

This jeer was so near the truth that Thea became still angrier. For she had often wished she could do more for the general poor, as it were, yet knew it to be impossible for her to do so. She replied coldly, therefore, her face set with distaste,

"Mr. Barrett, I have been prepared to advise you as far as I can about your personal affairs regarding Georgina, though I fear I can be of little help to you. However, I feel no obligation to discuss the injustices of the world with you, or the inadequacies of my sex; and so I would bid you good-day."

She rose to give him a distant curtsy, and as she did so, observed an awareness of his rudeness suddenly apparent in his face.

"Miss Langham, I crave your forgiveness. I cannot think what I have been about! Here you have given me so generously of your time and your help, and my only return is to abuse your sex. Though in truth it was not *you* I criticized!"

Thea's raised eyebrows and wide stare were sufficient to convey that she doubted the veracity of this statement, and she moved immediately toward the bell pull. So that it was with dismay that she found her path barred, and her hands clasped tightly in Miles Barrett's strong ones as he said impatiently, a deep cleft between his brows, a quite oversetting ferocity in his blue eyes,

"You must, you *will*, believe me! I cannot leave now, after your kindness, under your displeasure." And then quite gently, with a sudden warmth in his voice,

"Come, say you will forgive me! It is just that Annabel's hovel, the filthy tumble-down street, the ragged people, indeed the whole district, was so foul, so noisome, so . . . so terrible in every way. And yet the unhappy inhabitants had no means of helping themselves or improving it. And when I see our own spoilt beauties and affected dandies, and all the extravagances of the age, whether in France or here in England, I . . . well, I . . ."

Thea, with memories of her own heart-searching, her intermittent concern, as she now saw it, during the necessary exigencies of her own social life, looked at Miles Barrett and relented. She said, with considerably less vehemence,

"Indeed, sir, I am in complete accord with you. And yet, you know, there is really nothing we women can do, except the 'good deeds' you so despise. I am persuaded there are many in this country, gently reared certainly, sometimes indeed of the aristocracy, who are beginning to look with doubt, even horror, on our New Age. But I do not think—do you?—that a discussion, however spirited, of this sad situation will help us solve the more immediate problem of what you are to do about Georgina."

Miles Barrett began to laugh. He said, but not unpleasantly,

"Why, Miss Langham, you have a man's mind! However, to return as you suggest to our immediate problem: since you are convinced that my daughter loves me still despite my desertion, and would wish to be back in my charge, will you tell me, in your clearheaded way, what story you think—if indeed there is one—would be acceptable to Georgina and also satisfy our more worldly acquaintances here? That is, if they are not to upset her by whispering incredulously behind their fans! Then, perhaps, I can criticize or add to it, and between us we shall, hopefully, hammer out a passable . . . lie."

Thea, disliking this cynical tone, replied, a little coldy, that there was surely no need to lie. Or at least, she added in a sudden feminine fashion which brought another smile to her companion's face, not to fabricate *much*. All that seemed necessary, to her mind anyway, was to explain that Miles had fallen in with a friend who was very ill, somewhere sensibly more remote in Europe than France. He had remained, at this friend's request, until the end, which had been longer than expected.

"It is surely not necessary to mention the sex of this friend, except, of course, by innuendo that it was a man and not a woman," she continued.

Miles Barrett raised an eyebrow. "And why, then, did I not write to inform Humphrey, at least, of the situation?" he asked, sardonically.

"You did. But the letter, or letters, must have gone astray. The mails in England, to be sure, are good. But in, say, Spain or Italy, or Switzerland . . ."

"Capital! We shall have another Mrs. Radcliffe amongst us soon perhaps."

Thea flushed with a mixture of amusement and exasperation, but concluded with an attempt at coldness,

"From the little I have seen of you, you would seem capable of keeping your own counsel if you chose—and of giving a good set-down to anyone *presumptuous* enough to press for more details than you are prepared to give. As I collect, you have already seen your brother and sister-in-law without disclosing any information about where you have been these past months. It should therefore be child's play to you to give to the world the bare bones of such a story and no more. I realize there will be some talk, some speculation," she added, "but with no help from you to fan the flames, indeed, salutary dousing with cold water instead, this will soon die. And all Georgina need expect is a little curiosity which, with your backing, she should easily survive."

He looked at her seriously, his dark countenance a little flushed.

"It is an excellent notion, all the better for being, in essence, the truth. I shall take your advice, ma'am, and must thank you for it. I am sure I should have felt constrained for Georgina's sake to build a more elaborate structure—which would certainly never have held up."

Thea looked at him suspecting sarcasm but saw, instead,

a sincerity that seemed to make his saturnine countenance far more pleasing. Smiling, she held out her hand and said lightly,

"Well, that is all settled then. And I promise you your deep, dark secret will be safe with me. Now, can you not stay and take a little wine with my father? He would, I know, be glad to become better acquainted with you. And you need not fear his curiosity. He has none, except in scholarly matters."

Chapter 5

MR. *Langham, in his odd way, took a liking to Miles* Barrett. Thea, much amused, watched the growth of a friendship between two men far different in age and certainly in pursuits. Her father even when young had never, so she understood, shown the least tendency towards gaming, women, or any of the excesses Miles Barrett had, at some time or another, been renowned for. They did, however, have one firm common bond: they were both strongly for the Opposition, and above all concurred about the general industrial unrest, the near-famine and poverty and, though great landowners themselves, about the increase of the enclosure movement throughout the country. Indeed, as their world pursued its lighthearted way, they were often to be found deep in conversation on some such topic. It became the accepted thing that Miles Barrett and

Mr. Langham were earnest, both in their personal friendship and in their partisanship of His Majesty's government's Opposition.

At first, perhaps naturally, the *on-dit* was that Miles cleverly hoped to win the esteem of the so-detached Miss Langham through her father's good graces; for it was a well-known fact that Thea and her parent held each other in deep mutual affection and respect. But gradually even the most sanguine of gossips had to admit defeat, the whispering behind the fans ceased, and it became obvious to all that neither the beautiful, clever Miss Langham, nor the handsome, mysterious Mr. Barrett had any romantic interest in each other.

The surprise engendered by Miles's return suffered a similar fate: his carefully edited story, more or less accepted at first, had, with constant retelling, become old, threadbare stuff. With absolutely nothing further to gossip about—for Miles would seem to have become prodigiously dull and conventional—his past ceased to occupy anyone's thoughts.

So the days followed their even, pleasurable course. Maria Barton had long since returned to Lancashire. Thea had talked and danced a great deal, flirted a little, run her father's household, and charmed its guests as efficiently as ever. Georgina, happy now, living with her father and indulged in all the accomplishments, social, musical, and literary, that she could wish, had blossomed. All was, indeed, as it should be.

No one could know that, with the unexpected arrival of just one more handsome masculine face when most families had put up their town shutters and returned to the country, events would take a turn destined to alter radically many lives.

Oddly enough, it was Georgina who had first seen this new face only a day or so before leaving London. She was gazing contentedly through the carriage window as her father's coachman drove her back home to Bruton Street after a day spent happily with Lucy Dillingham, when she remarked a well-built young man of about twenty-five, handsome in a rather foreign fashion, leaning on his cane and waiting to cross the street. She would have been hard put to it, if asked, to explain what was particularly noteworthy about him. Perhaps it was just that his features were that much more well-defined, darker, handsomer, his clothes that much more perfect, his whole stance that much more elegant, than even the most dashing of all her new acquaintances. Not that he was in any way vulgar or ostentatious: he was just . . . *there,* and impressive in the extreme. She smiled to herself, and thought how she would present her First Vision of the Handsome Stranger to Lucy and Selina tomorrow. For, truth to tell, Georgina, though still a very nice girl, seemed to have moved a little too far, perhaps through reaction and heady change of circumstances, into the apparently empty-headedness of many of her contemporaries. Mrs. Dillingham and Thea, observing this with indulgent eyes, had decided that beneath the froth and flutter, Georgina was still as sound as she had ever been and that the pendulum would right itself in good time. Miles, as an indulgent father, had hardly noticed any transformation at all.

Rehearsing tomorrow's speech in her mind, Georgina looked back as the carriage passed in time to receive the full glance of a pair of dark, liquid, yet penetrating eyes. Her senses received a jolt quite out of proportion to the occasion or to the light, amusing story she was planning to tell. Flushed, her composure quite gone, she turned her face, now quite pretty under its elegant and becoming bonnet, forward again and drove the rest of the way home in a rather dazed state of mind. Next morning, for no reason she could well explain, she had her maid dress her hair in a very becoming mode, caught up behind, with tiny ringlets at each temple. She put on her best walking dress, in a very attractive shade of dark green, with a high military collar and frogs across the bodice. The style had been selected on the kindly advice of Thea, who had helped her choose her new wardrobe. Innocently aware of the charming picture she made, she had paused on the curved, elegant stone steps outside her father's house and looked to right and left before entering the carriage. But no breathtaking stranger observed her. Dimly she now realized that this was what she had hoped for, and so, feeling rather disconsolate, she waited to be driven as usual to the Dillinghams'. Moreover, she did not, curiously enough, tell her amusing First Vision story after all. Something, again for no very clear reason, restrained her, and she endured the Dillingham girls' harmless teasing about how grand she was looking that day with no word of explanation, and a foolish feeling of disappointment mingled with hope for the future in her heart.

But she had looked in vain for the handsome stranger during her few remaining days in London, surprised at her own silence about the small incident, for she was not at all secretive nowadays, and could hardly believe her feelings had been so affected by a brief glance that she should wish to keep them private. He never appeared again, and listen or inquire obliquely as she might, she had heard no talk of a newcomer or unexpected visitor in their dwindling London circle. Gradually he slipped away, first into the corners of her mind, then vanished altogether.

On her return to Lancashire with her father she found the weather to be still that of high summer. Frothy white clouds drifted across a porcelain sky, fresh, green, feathery leaves trembled in a soft breeze, the hedgerows were bright with color, the birds never ceased their chattering in the dewy mornings, or during the long, golden twilight. Very close by, to the east, lay green folds of hills, rising to desolate places; a little farther distant, streams rushed and tumbled down the deep cloughs which cut into the moors, and the still waters elsewhere reflected the sunlight.

All the same, Georgina found life dull after London. As one of the important families in this border area, she and her father had friends, certainly, and visited, picnicked, and dined, in normal fashion. But such entertainment as existed was sporadic, and anyway there happened to be, at that time, rather a disappointing dearth of young people in the district. Moreover, since neither hunting nor going out with the guns was in season, quite a number of people had left for Harrogate or Bath. Some, even more adventurous, had gone to Brighton, and those who stayed behind were, for the main part, occupied with the management of their estates, like Miles Barrett.

Still, there was one bright spot on the horizon, she reflected, for Thea was due to arrive to stay with her friend, Maria Barton, at Barton Hall within a sennight, and where Thea was, Georgina felt, no one could be dull. It was to be supposed that Maria would organize some sort of entertainment for her visiting friend, and as the two big houses, the Barretts' and the Bartons', were not far apart, Georgina could reasonably expect to be invited to several parties. Moreover, Thea was bringing Lucy and Selina Dilllingham with her.

She was riding out as usual in the extensive grounds of her father's house, reflecting on this rosier future, when her mount stumbled, and though no serious damage was done, Georgina thought it best to give the beast a little rest before returning home. She threw the bridle over a convenient root and walked a short distance to one of the boundary walls on the estate, where a small buttress, easy of access, supported the high wall alongside a leafy lane. This had been a favorite spot of hers long ago— before her mother's death, in fact—when she was allowed to run there with her nurse. Now, mounting easily onto the stone buttress, she was just able to see over the wall and sat quietly, lost in reverie. It was therefore only gradually that she became aware of the soft clip-clop of another mount outside on the lane and, looking up, found herself once again gazing directly into the eyes of her London Vision. Instinctively, because he had been so much in her thoughts earlier, she smiled shyly. But the stranger who, presumably, had no memory of *her,* looked first surprised, then gave a rather formal, confused bow. Georgina, naturally interpreting his reaction to mean that he had no idea who she was or why she should so obviously acknowledge him, said, a little breathlessly,

"Oh, I must beg your pardon! You do not remember me—indeed we have never met—but I remarked you from my father's carriage some weeks ago in London, as I was returning home to Bruton Street from a friend's."

This explanation could be said to sound a little odd. But perhaps the stranger's handsome looks had been the cause of other such vague acknowledgments in the past. His face cleared at once, and he seemed not at all surprised to have been recalled to mind in this fashion. He reined in close to the wall, and replied in a light, pleasant voice,

"Why, then, are you the daughter of Mr. Miles Barrett?" And as Georgina acknowledged this, added by way of explanation, "I am come to pay my respects to him, as I have lately taken a house on the far side of the village."

"That must be Yew Tree Mansion. I recollect having heard a new tenant has but recently arrived."

The stranger smiled. "It is indeed Yew Tree Mansion. And I arrived yesterday, to be precise. May I present myself? Jeremy Tregannan." He took Georgina's hand which she had extended prettily and a little shyly, saying as she did so, "Georgina Barrett."

Perhaps a more practiced, more sophisticated creature would have suspected a deliberate charm, a studied attempt to cultivate her interest as quickly and as surely as possible through such a chance meeting. But Georgina was still artless and trusting enough for no such thought to enter her head, and she was only charmed by her new acquaintance's frank open manner and handsome looks. Watching the slim, straight back of the stranger as he rode away, a delightful *frisson* of attraction and anticipation ran through her. She slid down from the buttress and, picking up the horse's bridle, made no attempt to mount, but walked slowly homeward, lost in a pleasant, silly, but harmless daydream of requited love.

Chapter 6

$SOME$ *few evenings later, Thea and Miles were idly dis-*
cussing the new tenant of Yew Tree Mansion, who had
called on Mr. Barrett as he had promised, the same day
he had encountered Georgina at the boundary wall. Thea
had yet to meet him, but expected to do so any minute,
since he had been invited by Miles to a small dinner that
evening to meet a few of his new neighbors. Invited also
were Lord and Lady Barton and their guest, Thea. Much
to Georgina's chagrin, she herself was not present, having
already a previous engagement with Selina and Lucy at a
young people's party nearby.

Some twenty minutes before the dinner hour, most
other guests were already present, seated comfortably,
yet with some formality, in Miles's elegant small drawing
room, which was decorated in the French fashion of an
earlier era. In common with other cultured Englishmen,

Miles, while still acceding to France's great decorative taste, disliked the more recent Empire mode, finding it often too florid. As the others were in small groups, conversation was not at the moment general, and Thea and Miles could therefore talk without difficulty. He shrugged impatiently.

"It's the devil! His manners, his address generally, everything about him, in fact, is impeccable, and yet I cannot feel much liking for him. Moreover, I have this . . . sensation of . . . familiarity, of having met him somewhere before . . . Yet he says emphatically that we have never encountered each other."

"Too emphatically?"

Miles reflected. "No. Just firmly disclaims any memory of such an encounter—although how he can be so sure is, perhaps, a little odd."

Thea's eyes laughed at him. "You seem to have remarkably little reason for taking him in dislike. Unless everything about him—barring, of course, his absolute certainty of not knowing you—is *too* perfect?"

Miles shook his head, smiling.

"No, he is quite unexceptionable. And yet—well, where does he come from? He has answered nothing to the purpose to any feelers I have thrown out. Certainly, his answers are all easy, and yet it is only natural that people place themselves, instinctively as it were, on first acquaintance. And everybody has *some* background, knows *someone*. Not that he evaded . . . Oh, I don't know. I am just not . . . easy . . . in my mind."

Although she understood fully what Miles was trying to convey, Thea could not resist saying with a laugh, "Why, I thought it was only silly, weak-minded females who had to rely on 'feelings' and 'intuition,' not the sterner sex!"

But to this Miles, laughing outright, had no time to reply, for the subject of their conversation was at that moment announced.

Surveying him critically yet discreetly through her long, thick lashes, Thea could on first sight find little to criticize in Jeremy Tregannan. He showed undoubted breeding, his manners were pleasant, open, yet discreet with the ladies of the party, and frank, often witty with the gentlemen. They were, perhaps, a little too studied, but in a distinguished, rather than *outré* fashion . . . rather, it came suddenly to Thea, like some of the French *émigrés* vaguely remembered from her far younger days. She pursued this thought, looking at the dark, handsome countenance with its short straight nose and liquid brown eyes. Indeed Mr. Tregannan could very likely be French, or at least of recent French antecedents. This could account, at least to some extent, for his lack of family background, if not of friends, here in England . . . She studied his dress. This, too, would seem to proclaim acquaintance with the best tailors, and was as restrained as Miles's own. Certainly, Mr. Tregannan would appear to be quite pleasingly normal and unexceptionable.

Having reached all these conclusions, Thea allowed Miles's uncertainties to slip from her mind and, on being seated at dinner, prepared to enjoy her companions on each side of her, both so far unknown. One was a middle-aged local squire, of High Church and Tory opinions, a fire-eater, yet obviously very good-hearted, whom she took to at once. The other was a slim young man whose father, it seemed, was but recently retired from the navy as a Rear Admiral, and had, with his considerable prize money, bought a large house in the district. Between the two of them, Thea was fully and pleasantly occupied, and unaware of any unusual controversy among the other guests, until suddenly Lady Barton's voice rose sharply, saying, with some emphasis, to her neighbor, a fine-drawn, quiet middle-aged man, with yet something military about him,

"I do assure you, it is not that I am a . . . a renegade to my upbringing! It is just that, well, when I saw their faces . . . like corpses . . . and the way they looked at us as we drove through that dreadful Manchester slum, I was not only terrified, but *sorry* for them! How terrible to live so! And," she added in low tones, "for us to be hated so! It made me think of the old French aristocracy!"

Both the manner and matter of this statement from the conventional, Junoesque Lady Barton naturally had the effect of stopping all other conversation. And at this Maria, looking extremely handsome with a high, yet beautiful flush on her countenance, subsided somewhat, regaining sufficient control of herself to give her attention to Thea's nice squire, who spoke soothingly to her across the table.

"Your pity does you credit, my dear. But every man has his appointed place in this world. The best *we* can do is look after our own tenantry, and that's that."

"But they had no one to look after them! They were townsfolk, many of them, with no skills, nor means of finding work. Or, at best, poor craftsmen, whom these new factories are supplanting."

Thea was aware, in that moment, of a strange, sweeping glance from the unexpectedly glittering eyes of Jeremy

Tregannan, before he dropped his heavy lids over them.
And of the fact that, in contrast to this covert, momentary,
yet almost sinister look, his hand continued to twirl his
wine glass lightly, casually . . . A man of parts, and a
deep one, she decided swiftly, before giving her attention
again to the tide of conversation and opinion that Lady
Barton's remark had occasioned. The languid young man
on her left was saying, foolishly, that such creatures—
presumably the evil-looking poor—should be flogged,
though precisely why, he did not explain. Perhaps, it
occurred to Thea, for having the insolence to stare at
an elegant carriage. And now, at this reflection, there
rose unexpectedly in her mind an incident she had
chanced to witness years ago in Bath, of a huge, ragged
specimen of a man caught redhanded stealing from a stall
as her parents' heavy carriage was rumbling past. She
must have been about thirteen at the time, seated safe
within, between her mother and her governess, but the
vehicle had been forced to stop, and she had never forgotten how the man had thrown up his tousled head and
shouted in a coarse voice, pointing at theirs—the nearest
—carriage:

"Aye, and I'd *kill* you if I could! No work, no food at
home, the bairns dying, bread the price it is! What's to
become of us—of *me*—now?"

He would have been deported, or even hanged, she
reflected, sadly. Impatient with the young man beside
her still pursuing his vague threats, first against the
poverty-stricken generally, and then against the fire
raisers and machine breakers who were again active,
though not in their part of the world, she in turn said in
low yet angry tones,

"It is quite foolish to speak so, sir. Such people are human, you know, not naturally violent, and probably as reasonable as us, if they could but find work. But today, with poor wages, enclosures, and machinery, it is not only their livelihood, but their very lives they are fighting for. What else can they do—ignorant, unlettered and without guidance or protection as they mostly are—but plot and break machines, fire-raise, steal, and threaten? Especially," she added recklessly, "when they see our expensive Prince amusing himself while a large body of the country starves."

In return for this speech she received a wide stare of such utter incomprehension that, if she could not still see the vision of that wild, tortured face from years ago, she would have laughed. As it was, perhaps it was better that her listener did not understand: he would have thought her not only mad, like the poor old King, but *traitorously* so. On this reflection, she glanced up to realize that her voice, though low, must have been more penetrating than she had intended. Miles Barrett was looking hard at her from his place beyond her immediate circle, an indefinable expression, now, on *his* face; and directly opposite, Jeremy Tregannan's sharp eyes met her surprised gaze until, as before, he looked away and, again twirling his glass, said lightly,

"Come, come, Miss Langham, so beautiful, so fierce, and—a little disloyal?"

It was fortunate, with such deliberate provocation, that Miles at this point obviously decided that tempers were running too high, and things said that should not have been, however close and friendly a group they were—except for the new tenant at Yew Tree Mansion. He remarked, plaintively, that such controversies were extremely harmful to the digestion, and as his housekeeper, Mrs. Horrocks, and Cook would be in a great taking if the game pies and savory patties were not eaten and appreciated, let alone the jellies and puddings, everyone must desist from such argument.

His good humor and a skillful reference to modern France, again, perhaps, about to become the common enemy, had the desired effect, and everyone, undoubtedly relieved, hastily and obligingly turned to other topics of conversation. Except the stranger, who said nothing.

Was he, Thea wondered, eying him covertly and uneasily, a government informer? There were, she knew, many such government spies these days, alert for any supposed disloyalty to realm or throne. Though not usually, she was forced to admit, in her circle of life.

Chapter 7

*THE weather continued fine and warm, and Mr. Lang*ham was abroad on family business in Italy; there was a brief outbreak of summer sickness not only in London, but also in her home county of Surrey, so Thea needed very little pressing from Maria and William Barton to remain longer with them in Lancashire. Mrs. Dillingham having willingly written her consent, Lucy and Selina too were delighted to remain with their elder sister, who was far more indulgent with them than their Mama, and treated them much more as the young ladies they both considered themselves to be.

The Barton family and their guests, and Miles Barrett and his daughter, thus began to see a good deal of each other. The three young girls quite naturally gravitated to one another, and Thea, with Maria and William, enjoyed the company of Miles Barrett. Indeed it seemed that almost every day some meeting or excursion was arranged, and although frequently neither Miles nor William could attend, being occupied with business on their estates, other families now returned to the area were most anxious to do so. The gentlemen among them seemingly had more leisure, so that the expeditions never lacked for company. Thea (rather than Maria, who was perhaps too casual), keeping a firm eye on the three younger girls, was amused to find the Rear Admiral's son much smitten with Lucy, whose blonde vivacity apparently charmed him to a degree. Selina too, was much in demand, whereas Georgina, to Thea's surprise, although universally liked, did not "take" as either of the Dillingham sisters had done. This was partly, she suspected, because her young companion, though always pleasant, appeared to take no special interest in other people or their affairs: as Thea had long known, the best, perhaps the only way, to a young gentleman's heart was through a seemingly insatiable interest in him—his problems, occupations, likes and dislikes.

Thea herself was amused to find a certain Major Hodson in pursuit of her, but in so noble and soldierly a fashion that she could take no exception to him. While taking care not to encourage any hopes in his heart, she enjoyed his company well enough, especially as he had informed her that though at present on indefinite leave from his regiment, he was expecting to be recalled in the near future. She found Miles Barrett pleasant, too, amusing, knowledgeable, sensitive to people and surroundings, and with a very real concern for his land, his tenants, and his estates generally.

Indeed, the only member of the company now not to her taste was Jeremy Tregannan. Yet why, she could not tell. He continued to be unfailing, pleasant company, easy yet never overfamiliar with the younger girls; and was especially courteous and careful with Georgina, who at first appeared to have developed an innocent crush on him, but afterward, when he showed no sign of reacting to this, relapsed into an indifference sometimes verging almost on rudeness. Recalling Miles's remarks about him and determined not to be influenced by them, Thea often, walking, talking, riding, even dancing with him, attempted inwardly to account for her dislike . . . distrust . . . she knew not what to call it. She kept repeating to herself that he was helpful, amusing, interesting, reliable, unexceptionable in his manner, his goodwill distributed, as it were, throughout the company, among both male and female friends—and yet still she could not like him.

She had naturally, however, thought this attitude unobserved, for she had been long enough in the world to look one thing and think another. So it was with an acute shock, as they were riding one morning in a party along the high lanes near the Yorkshire borders, that she found him alongside her and maneuvering to fall back a little from the other riders until he was able to say, with a sudden unaccustomed, shy charm that greatly became him,

"Miss Langham, I . . . I cannot think why you have so taken me in dislike!"

As, of necessity, she turned her head to refute this statement, he continued in a low tone, quite lacking his usual resilient manner,

"No, I beg you not to perjure yourself, nor embarrass either of us further than I have done already in speaking so! For it would do no good; I know it for a fact that almost from our very first meeting, you . . . you were not anxious to continue our acquaintance. And yet . . . I am at a loss why."

As Thea well knew, so was she. Impossible to quote Dr. Fell at him, yet equally impossible to refute what he had just said.

She therefore drew rein, so that the two of them fell still farther behind the others, and regarding him levelly with her calm, beautiful eyes, answered him in absolute sincerity.

"I must be honest—since you have so obviously divined something of my attitude that cannot be refuted—and tell you, frankly, that I don't know. It has worried me . . ." She paused wondering how best to conclude this extraordinary conversation and extricate herself from it as quickly as might be. But as he continued to say nothing, only regarding her with a serious, unwavering stare, she stumbled on, angry at her own unaccustomed gaucherie and at his ill manners in precipitating such a situation,

"I mislike mysteries, I suppose. And to me, I must admit, you seem such: never open about yourself. Also, if you will forgive me, you would seem to me to . . . to *watch* us—*observe* us so carefully!" And then seeing what appeared to be utter astonishment in his gaze, she went on quickly.

"I am sure this is all a hum, and my mind is too active through my present lazy existence. It is just that you never speak of your relatives, your home, or even your friends . . . I am not suggesting," she lifted an eyebrow with a flash of her normal humor, "that one must know your antecedents before accepting you as a friend—we are not, after all, living in the eighteenth century—but *everyone*, from Gentleman Jackson to Harriet Wilson, has friends, relatives, a *background*, of whatever sort, and none the worse for it. Only *you* have not . . ." She ended hastily, yet with spirit,

"I apologize if I have given you offense. But you will collect, it was *you* who began this astonishing and unedifying conversation."

She knew not what to expect, an outburst of offended dignity, perhaps, which would have been quite permissible in the circumstances, and wished at that moment with all her heart that she had not been so outspoken.

But instead, to her utter amazement, he merely dismissed all her utterances with a casual wave of his hand (which did not endear him any further to her) and asked instead, considerably at a tangent,

"Are you alone in this feeling of, shall we say, discomfort in my presence, Miss Langham? Or . . . forgive me, but Miles Barrett, for instance, whom I know to be a great friend, at least, of yours . . . he feels as you do? He has, perhaps, even mentioned me to you?"

This was more than Thea could stomach. She answered shortly, with all her previous discomfiture forgotten, her color rising, and a wide look from her expressive eyes that, had she known it, caused Jeremy Tregannan's head to spin.

"Sir, this is incredible! You go too far! My feelings are my own, and I do not go about discussing them. Ask Mr. Barrett himself, or anyone else you wish, if you are illbred enough, any such questions. But I beg you will not attempt to embarrass me further with your queries. And now, if you will excuse me, I must rejoin the others. We shall soon cause comment."

Spurring her mare forward, she was quickly and unobtrusively among the main body of riders again—and took
care to avoid her enigmatic inquisitor from then onward.

The next afternoon it was wet, and sitting *à trois* in
the small salon with Maria and William, Thea was so
abstracted as to cause comment. Maria wondered if she
were ill or at least sickening with something, and William,
always rather overly careful with his health, though exceedingly kind, opined that too many excursions in the
open air, now that she and Maria were no longer young,
were obviously taking their toll. But, still pondering her
conversation with Mr. Tregannan, Thea was not even
sufficiently distracted or amused by this remark to point
out that twenty-six, though certainly not the first bloom
of youth, was not yet senile either.

Fortunately this depressing dialogue between husband
and wife was interrupted by the arrival of Miles Barrett.
He had been riding past after a visit to the scene of a small
flood a few miles away and, recalling that Georgina was
still with Lucy and Selina at the Bartons', he had decided
to collect her himself in his light carriage instead of sending the heavy coach and groom for her later, when the
weather and roads might have deteriorated further.
Nothing loth, he sat down at their invitation to take tea
with them, the damp and sudden late afternoon chill having made the offer doubly welcome. As it fell out, William
was going to collect a parish document he wished Miles
to look at, and Maria was momentarily occupied with a
servant's query. Thea, therefore took the opportunity to
mention, briefly, her odd conversation with Jeremy
Tregannan the previous morning. But Miles, first mildly

surprised, then rather grave, had no time for discussion, as the Bartons returned just as Thea finished her account. On leaving, however, he contrived privately to suggest that she should ride over with Lucy and Selina the following morning—Maria always being occupied with household affairs or her young child at this time. He would arrange to be at home, instead of out on business, so that Thea could speak privately with him, more explicitly, about what was said by Mr. Tregannan.

This was accordingly accomplished, and the next morning found the two of them once again cudgelling their brains about the stranger. Miles was even more certain now that he had met the man before somewhere . . . but could not think where . . . Thea, weary after part of the night spent puzzling on the matter and trying unsuccessfully to think of anyone who might have knowledge of him, suddenly recalled, forcibly, that he had made no attempt yesterday even to 'place' himself, either geographically, as it were, or socially, after her criticism.

"And yet, you know, one cannot ask him *outright*," Miles answered this observation. "Anyway, it would do no good. The only remote lead we have, which I collect now not to have told you, is that he implied, some time ago, that he had French antecedents. But how the deuce can one check there, with so many poor devils dead, their heads severed from their necks these many long years? And with the émigré population here scattered now— and from so many diverse parts of France, anyway . . . ?"

"It would not matter so much," Thea pursued her own train of thought, "if one did not sense him to have come here *for a purpose*. Why here? And for what?"

"Well, he must live somewhere, I suppose," replied Miles, reasonably.

"Yes, but consider the sequence of events, Miles. First, Georgina notices him in town, near your house in Bruton Street. Then he arrives here, settles into a rented mansion, and continues by making your acquaintance—and now, is seldom away from your doorstep. There are too many coincidental encounters. Almost as though you, at least, are being stalked! Has he been away at all since his arrival here over two months ago? No. Has he had any friends to visit him? No. Have we even encountered him with some acquaintance not met through us? No. Has *anyone* ever said, 'We are already known to each other,' or 'We have a mutual friend in so-and-so'—everyday happenings in our world! No!"

"Here, steady, my dear Thea! You will have me calling the Thief Takers next!"

Thea laughed: put that way, her fears did indeed sound melodramatic. And morning callers being announced, and Selina, Lucy, and Georgina descending with the newest copy of La Belle Assemblée, the matter was allowed to drop.

That it would not have been so allowed, however, was certain if Miles, or Thea, or the Bartons, or, indeed, any of their friends, had known of an affair prospering clandestinely behind their backs: for all the fact that Jeremy Tregannan appeared as happily indifferent to Georgina as to any other young ladies in the area, and that Georgina herself even seemed sometimes to have actually taken him in dislike after her earlier penchant for him, this was but a facade. Georgina and Jeremy were, in fact, deep in an affair, and her infatuation was so great, that he had even succeeded in schooling her to show no hint of her feelings whatsoever. The fact that she was not normally deceitful by nature, but frank, sunny, prone nowadays, even, to be too open in her regard and her emotions, served only to emphasize the depth of those she had for Jeremy. But no one knew. Neither Lucy, nor Selina had heard a whisper or a hint, and suspected nothing. And where they, as bosom friends of the same age, had no inkling, how could anyone else be expected to know about such a state of affairs?

Chapter 8

ALTHOUGH the weather was now changeable, the days passed pleasantly by until Thea, knowing her father's return to Surrey from Italy to be imminent, decided she must leave her good friends and return to the pleasant, commodious house she dwelt in with her father in the little village of Ewell. However, although her maid was already packing, she was persuaded to remain for just five nights more so that she could attend a spectacular grand ball Lord Bowland was giving at his seat, not too far distant. Selina and Lucy (like Georgina) were, of course, too young to go, being not yet out, and consequently were allowed to attend only small, local parties. They were happy, all the same, to remain a little longer at Maria's, and begged Thea to tell them especially if the spectacular new gas lighting in the grand ballroom was all it was puffed up to be. It was known Prinny himself would not be there, as he was otherwise occupied, but two of his brothers, the Dukes of York and Clarence, were to attend (and Thea had a soft spot for the bluff sailor prince). It was also rumored that other oddly assorted guests might include Lord Byron and even (the Prince Regent not being present) the Beau himself. Altogether, according to gossip, it sounded a stimulating as well as a fashionable affair, and Thea, who liked both Beau Brummell and his wit, though she had little time for Lord Byron, decided willingly to put off her journey until the following week.

Thea was, then, in her bedroom on the evening before that of the ball, sitting up over a dying fire and one of Miss Austen's romances, long after the rest of the house had settled for sleep, when she thought to hear sounds, though muffled by the thick curtains, of light, furtive footsteps on the gravel two floors below. Uncertain, thinking herself of necessity mistaken, she laid by her book, but further scuffling noises, as if someone frantically hurried, brought her quickly to the window, and slipping between the drapes and the window embrasure, she looked down, attempting to see who was there. But the moon, although up, was fitful, and all she could discern was a vague impression of a female figure half running, half stumbling, the back bowed as though under considerable strain or distress, turning the corner to the servants' wing.

It passed through her mind that one of the maids, perhaps, had broken rules and was anxiously attempting to return unnoticed. But something, some impression of wildness or grief or worry about the figure, remained with her, so that wrapping her robe more firmly round her bedgown, she caught up the night light and left the room silently, making her way in the direction of the servants' stairs, and yet with no firm idea what she would do if she caught the culprit red-handed, as it were.

She need not have worried, however; well before she reached the servants' wing, on a turn of the wide oak stair into the first-floor corridor, the cloaked figure literally ran into her, with a cry of fright and dismay: Georgina. Both women remained frozen, thinking the cry had perhaps been heard. But no one stirred, and Thea, feeling the chilled, gloveless hands of the miscreant, and the dampness of her pelisse, (for a light rain had been falling earlier), put a finger to her lips, and drew the girl along to her own bedchamber. There, pushing her into the chair where she herself had but lately sat reading, and throwing a bright red shawl which was to hand around her, she made up the fire into a healthy blaze again. Only then, she turned to Georgina for an explanation, to find her sitting with her head in her hands, shoulders silently shaking, and huge tears running between her fingers and down her wrists onto the brilliant shawl. Thea herself was too worried to be angry, and there was such desolation in the girl's attitude that, kneeling in front of her, carefully pulling off the damp pelisse and rearranging the shawl, she asked as gently as she could,

"Georgina, my dear, what are you doing here in this house—instead of at home? Where have you been? And what is the matter? You *must* tell me," she added in firmer tones, as these queries evoked no response except more racking sobs, "or I shall have to rouse Lord Barton to send over for your father at once."

Two huge red-rimmed eyes peered at her in horror. "Oh! No, no! I . . . I came to you . . . To get your help! I . . . I was on my way back there, you see, but suddenly I . . . I couldn't go any farther . . ."

This made no sense to Thea who asked, not unnaturally, "You mean you were on your way back to your *father's house?* But why were you out, alone?" only to be interrupted by a cry of,

"Oh, will you not *try* to understand? I was safe back there at Father's, you see, when I remembered my reticule and went out again!"

"You had better tell me the whole story. *Coherently,* Georgina. I cannot help you, nor advise you, if you talk in riddles. And I shall pass no comment, until you have concluded your story." It was on the tip of Thea's tongue to say "no judgment," but she refrained since the girl was so obviously beside herself.

At this, and at the firm, almost bracing tone noted in Thea's voice, the worst of Georgina's hysteria left her. She drew a long sigh and said in a low, but unsteady voice,

"I have been seeing Jeremy Tregannan. Regularly. We are in love," this with a touch of defiance, but Thea schooled herself to make no sign. "We meet in a small," the young voice faltered, "well, I *suppose* it is a deserted house, but one room is cosily, nay elegantly, furnished . . . although I collect the hall and stairway are carpetless and empty, and some of the windows boarded . . . Anyway, it is but a short distance north of here and not above two miles, by side tracks, from my home."

Thea waited, her heart racing, but her face expressionless. Georgina, perhaps unnerved at this very immobility, hurried on,

"We . . ." her voice shook, "we but *meet,* Thea! Jeremy waits with his light carriage outside our boundary

wall—there's a buttress there I used to climb as a child—
and then he drives me to this house, and we," again the
shaky voice, "usually we kiss and . . . and hold hands
and talk. That, I tell you, is *all!* And then, afterward,
he drives me back to the same spot, and helps me over
the wall . . . It is but three minutes through the grounds
to the house from there."

Resisting an impulse to demand why, if the circumstances were so innocent, such clandestine behavior was
necessary, and to point out that Miles Barrett could at
least have been asked if Jeremy could pay court to his
daughter, however young she might be (or had Miles
already refused? she wondered suddenly), Thea merely
asked, in the level tones that seemed best to control
Georgina's hysteria,

"Did you behave so tonight?" And receiving a brief,
furtive nod in reply, continued, "So why, if, as I collect
you said earlier, you were already back in your father's
house, and Jeremy presumably ridden off, did you venture
out again, on foot, and such a distance? Am I *really* to
understand you were returning to . . . that curious house
simply to collect a reticule?" Another nod. "But you
became afraid for some reason and came to find me,
instead."

"Yes," said Georgina, through trembling lips. "I dare
not saddle Beauty for fear of discovery. But I *had* to
reclaim my property!" Her hands, now, began to shake
and twist too, so that Thea, foreseeing serious hysteria,
and deciding to leave the reason for such secrecy for a
later time, said swiftly,

"I have but two more questions for you at the moment,
Georgina. Firstly, exactly why were you returning to the

rendezvous—I cannot accept the excuse of a mislaid reticule. And secondly, how are you able to get into this house . . . or, for that matter, in and out of your father's —with such ease?"

The first question, Thea felt to be by far the most important, but she hoped, by linking it to the other purely practical one, that Georgina's answer would be more coherent, more complete, perhaps more forthright. And in this she was correct.

"I . . . I left my reticule on the love seat, and it had letters, love letters, from Jeremy, a monogrammed hand-kerchief, a . . . a special ring, my engraved vinaigrette— things unmistakably mine in it, and I thought—I *know*—it would be discovered before I met Jeremy there again . . . We only meet occasionally, you see."

Thea experienced a curious prickling sensation at the base of her neck.

"But *why* should it be 'discovered' as you put it? You have already said you are almost certain the house is deserted. Besides, you have only to ask your . . . beloved" (she could not keep a little of her distaste for the entire business from slipping into her voice, and Georgina flushed) "to collect it for you—you will probably see him tomorrow. Or even if not, you could reach him by mes-senger to ask him to do so."

There was a long pause. Then Georgina, who had been inexplicably shaking her head towards the end of this speech, lifted wholly candid eyes to Thea and said, simply,

"We are not the only visitors. Other people meet there too. Not women. Men. I heard two or three of them once, in the hall, and Jeremy was angry with them for coming unannounced or something. And once there were papers and books and things, in disarray, on the desk, that Jeremy shut quickly away. I imagine he thought I didn't notice . . . and that I am more . . . foolish . . . than I am. But I *love* him so. And he loves me. I am *convinced* of it."

Into the studied silence, she continued,

"You see, he is gone away for two days—he told me so tonight. And I am afraid in case these men will go there again before he returns—and certainly before I can reach him—they will find my wretched reticule; and he will not be there to save it, or me, if they should wish to make use of it in some way . . . to blackmail us, perhaps. Oh, how I wish I knew who they were! They may be harmless, true. But . . . they sounded so rough . . . they may, as well, be utterly unscrupulous!"

Now, as she spoke, she rose, so agitated that the shawl caught at her and she almost fell. Clutching Thea convulsively, she sobbed over and over again, begging her to accompany her to collect her property. "With you beside me, I can do it. Alone, I *cannot!* I am too tired, too *frightened!*" Here, she broke down utterly.

Thea's mind was in a whirl, trying to work out various possibilities and, despite herself, pitying Georgina for her youth and her panic.

"I am still at a loss about your means of entry and egress. I can only suppose you carry keys like a housekeeper, to your own house, to this one, and to your . . . your unsavory-sounding trysting place."

Her sarcasm had the hoped-for effect. Georgina calmed herself and answered explicitly,

"I use the garden door at home, behind the flower room. Everyone thinks it has only one key and is permanently locked; here, at Lord Barton's, I swear to you, I *chanced* to find the pantry door open. I was too distracted to have thought of how to get to you so late; and I was fortunate—perhaps some servant is out . . ." She added finally, in an agonized whisper,

"The . . . the other house has a key permanently hidden . . . in the eaves above the back porch. Jeremy used it once, when he had misplaced his own. I suppose it is there so that the . . . the others can get in if need be."

The pause lengthened. Thea looked at Georgina, such a strange mixture of innocence and guile, of stupidity and shrewdness as she had turned out to be, and now utterly to pieces. She said slowly,

"I cannot decide, Georgina, what to do about this. Your father will have to be told, there is no doubt of it; I will not be a party to such deception on your part, for I have little doubt you have not even sought his advice on the advisability of Jeremy Tregannan as a suitor."

Georgina shook her head, utterly distracted,

"No! Jeremy said . . ."

"I have no interest in what Mr. Tregannan said. What *I* was about to say was that your father must be told; but not, I think tonight. I shall take you up on my mare—that is, if we can leave here unobserved—deposit you at your own home and then myself ride over to this house, whose exact location you will give me, and collect your foolish reticule." She added, more to herself than to Georgina,

"If Mr. Tregannan is away, and you have had a rendezvous already so late, there is little likelihood or danger of my running into either him or his strange friends; although

I shall take good care before venturing into the house at all."

For a brief moment Georgina pleaded to be allowed to accompany her, but Thea would have none of it: Georgina would be but a hindrance in her present state. Anyway, truth to tell, Thea thought to discern, through the girl's protestations, a vast relief at having her unpleasant task done for her, with no further exertion on her part. Some short while later, therefore, dressed warmly, and with Georgina attired in a dry gown and cloak of Thea's, the two of them were successful in leading Thea's mare quietly from her stable, (fortunately a little apart from the main block, and reserved especially for visitors' mounts), and getting clear away from the house without discovery. Then, after a brief gallop to Miles's house, waiting only to observe Georgina scale her own boundary wall and signal briefly by means of a candle that she was safe within the house, Thea set off on her hazardous and lonely journey.

Chapter 9

IT occurred to Thea, as she rode along, keeping to the verges where the narrow route was too muddy or too stony—Georgina had, at least, described the way fully and coherently—that she would have done better perhaps to rouse her own coachman to attend her. He was the soul of discretion, loyal, and had known her since she was in leading strings. But she was uncertain of his exact sleeping quarters and fearful of rousing the household, who could not be relied upon not to gossip, and whose loyalties would, anyway, lie elsewhere. If the problem had been merely that of a lost reticule, she reflected, she would have bothered not at all to collect it, and for all Thea cared in her present anger, Georgina could have faced the consequences of its whereabouts and of Miles's wrath, along with Jeremy Tregannan when he returned. But the curious story of the strange visitors and the hidden key, the desk littered with papers hastily concealed, and her over-all suspicion of Jeremy—all this savored of conspiracy and danger, and the less known openly of it, the better. People in authority would have to be told, but secretly, so as to avoid alerting any wrongdoers; and it would, anyway, be far better if the silly child's belongings were not left in evidence for either plotters (if they were such) or honest investigators to find. Georgina's name must, if possible, be kept out of the affair.

These and various other thoughts ran pell-mell through her mind, until she found herself facing the large, thick copse that, according to Georgina lay between the house and the slippery track she had just ridden along. She drew rein, wondering if it would be best to dismount at once and approach through the trees, or ride a little longer skirting the wood, and then, hiding her mare just within the copse, make the final approach on foot beyond the trees. She decided on the latter course, knowing her long riding habit would hamper her considerably in a tramp through the thick tangled undergrowth and so, hoping there were no outposts, or sentries, or anything so dramatic to observe her progress, she cantered softly round the perimeter. Eventually reining in, she tied Silver, her mare, to the stoutest near-by tree she could find just within the copse, leaving her contentedly cropping the little grass that remained before fern, pine needles, and dead undergrowth covered the ground. Ahead of her stood the house, steep-gabled, utterly dark, sinister with its blind, mostly boarded windows. There was no moon, but the rain clouds had cleared at least temporarily, the stars were out, and the night light enough for her to make out a wild, bedraggled hedge, a wicket gate badly askew and, beneath a

porch untidy with tangled climbing briars, a heavy studded
front door. But the key, she remembered, was under the
back eaves. Her skirt swished gently in the long, rank
grass, and the hem and her petticoats were now so wet
that the damp had risen above her riding boots and felt
moist against her knees. She made her way cautiously
round the outside of the hedge to the back of the house.
Here, a short cottage porch sloped down over an equally
heavy door, and ramshackle guttering, choked with long
dead leaves, edged it: this, then, must be where the key was
to be found.

Thea stood stock still for several seconds, but apart from
a pheasant's sudden squawk, which almost sent her
stumbling away at speed, nothing stirred; with a grimace
of distaste she walked through the aperture in the hedge,
(this gate had long since gone), and pulling off her thick
glove stepped forward to fumble among the heavily wet,
decayed leaves for the key, reflecting as she did so that it
was a good thing she was tall: a smaller person would
have needed a stool, or such like, to search so. Illogically,
she wondered if all the eerie visitors were tall, or whether
they came together, and the smaller could rely on the taller
to obtain entry. But the vision conjured up was so
nightmarish that her fingers having closed round the
large, old-fashioned, and exceedingly heavy key at last,
she hastily placed it in the lock, turned it, and pushed the
door open soundlessly onto utter blackness.

Attempting to steady her nerves by reflecting logically
that secrecy must, indeed, be intended if hinges and lock
were so well oiled, Thea closed the door behind her and
again stood immobile. Again nothing moved. The house
had that indefinable yet certain quality of being deserted;

so deserted, indeed, that she felt she would have welcomed a scurrying of mice, perhaps, as a sign of another living thing in the deadness. (But, obviously, if the house were visited regularly, the mice had learned to keep away, too, when locks turned and doors opened.) With shaking fingers, Thea lit the small night lantern she had brought with her and, following Georgina's instructions, turned at once to the first door on the right, opening it cautiously to make certain the shutters were closed. Having ascertained this, she lifted the lamp higher, and hastily drawing the thick drapes across the closed shutters as an additional precaution against discovery, turned to observe the room. It was indeed both elegant and comfortable: a pale blue watered silk paper adorned the walls, there were several elegant yet comfortable chairs, an exquisite Sheraton side table holding a decorative oil lamp, thick Persian rugs, and above the graceful fireplace, where the dead remains of a fire were still in evidence, an unmistakable marine painting by Turner.

But while, as it were, absorbing these articles, Thea's eyes passed over a delicate japanned chair with a painted Chinese panel, and fell at once on the love seat next to it, where Georgina claimed to have left her reticule: and there, indeed, it was. With a gasp of relief, Thea caught it up, slung it tight on her wrist, and started to hurry from the room intent only on escape. But then the desk caught her eye—closed, no papers visible, seemingly harmless, possibly empty; unaccountably, her curiosity got the better of her fear and she moved quietly over to it.

It was locked. The long center drawer, the four small side ones, all refused to yield to her tugs, so that there remained only the apparently immovable ridge along the back of the desk, as a possible secret drawer. If Thea had not possessed just such a desk herself, considered a rarity, she would never have known of such a possible hiding place; as it was, she slipped an unseen catch and saw, with mixed feelings, the narrow aperture within.

So absorbed was she, sliding her fingers downwards to encounter, tantalizingly, the very edge of several papers, that she hardly heard the soft rustlings until, growing louder, they became identifiable as footsteps approaching cautiously through the long grass beyond the hedge. Her body stiffened; her fingers turned to ice. Almost without thought, she flicked the solid ridge into place, having discovered nothing of the contents of the papers, pulled back the curtains she had recently drawn across, and hurried to the door.

But the soft footsteps were already padding up the little path: impossible to get away now. Her mind working automatically, she shut the sitting room door behind her and took to the bare, rickety stairs upwards trying, by keeping to the edges, to avoid telltale footprints in the dust. At the top, near a turn in the stairway as soon as she safely might, she doused her light. And only then, as she stood there rigid, did she realize the key was still clutched in her hand. The door remained closed, the nocturnal visitor on the far side of it, presumably searching for the means of entry. Through her panic, she became aware now of voices, one soft, with a curious North country flatness of vowel, yet with an Irish lilt, saying, mildly exasperated,

"Bedamn these leaves, take you till Judgment Day to fish the bloody key out!"

And then another, rougher, unmistakably English, with a hard whine to it, a Cockney or Southerner of some sort,

"No need to bother anyway. Here's his Nibs's nag, if I hears right. He'll open with his own key. Best stand and wait, and *try*, Mick, to look civil! He's a havey-cavey kind of fellow, for all his sweet tongue, and don't you forget it!"

There was a grunt, or a snicker, in reply to this, and then, unmistakably, the clip clop of hooves, softened, certainly, but riding right up the little path to the back door. A voice, educated this time but, try as she might, unidentifiable through the thick wood of the door (and, perhaps, because of her own beating heart), said equably,

"Good-evening to you. Tie the beast to this post, will you?" and then, "But first, the password and signs, if you please."

"Aw, Sorr," came the soft-voiced drawl, "No need fer that between us, surely now? We're known to each other!"

"Nevertheless," through the teeth, "some of us, from other areas, for instance, are *not* known . . . and others —I would have you reflect on this *grimly*, Michael—are not what we seem, being instead spies, informers, agents provocateurs even. And if such were to get wind of our plans, whatever they be, it would be necessary to change signs, or password, or both. If, that is, we stayed free to tell the tale . . ."

There was a vague, soft, seemingly resentful mutter, followed at once by the educated, incisive voice replying,

"Well then, you will understand it now. And you will get into the *habit* of both signs and passes. Even with your own mother, you fool, or your own dog, if they purport to be one of us. So—shall we begin again?"

The deadly venom now in the cultured voice turned Thea's knees to water. She heard no password. Or rather perhaps, took no heed of it. And, of course, saw no signs, whatever that might mean. But crouched against the upstairs wall, she heard the door open and had sufficient wit left to reflect that at least the newcomer had used his own key, and her theft of that from the eaves was, so far at least, undiscovered. What sounded to be three pairs of feet marched across the hall and into the room she had just left so hastily, the soft voice, incorrigible, saying curiously,

"I thought you were off to the Dales for a night or so, Sorr. Couldn't quite fathom when I got the signal tonight. Nor Jem here couldn't, neither."

"I was so. But then I got word that two brethren from Yorkshire were travelling òver, expecting to rendezvous here in the early hours with . . . oh, God knows, some news, or plans . . ." The speaker had perhaps thought better of saying too much himself. The door to the prettily furnished room shut. The voices became an indistinguishable murmur.

After a minute or two, Thea eased her cramped limbs and looked about her. Ahead, at the end of a narrow, dirty, carpetless passage, a door stood ajar, faint starlight shining through the aperture. If she could, without noise, enter and make for the window there, she thought, she would gain the two-fold advantage of perhaps observing the expected "brethren's" faces, and, more important, of knowing when it would be safe to leave, by watching the entire group themselves quitting the house. That one of these was Jeremy Tregannan she was now certain. She had heard his voice often enough in drawing rooms, on pleasure expeditions, at dinner tables, and just now, raised, when he had entered the house—there was no mistaking it.

The horror of it all, and her responsibility to learn as much as possible, almost overcame her. She debated creeping down to listen outside the door to the little sitting room but that, she sensibly decided, would be both foolhardy and reckless. She would undoubtedly be caught: apart from the fact that the stairs creaked abominably, she would have nowhere to hide should the door open, or a sudden knock on the outer door betoken the newcomers from Yorkshire. No, she would do better to remain where she was, and learn what she could while staying safe to inform the authorities later.

The room she managed to enter silently, was, like the hall below and the corridor, empty, dirty, and with peeling, scrofulous walls. Fortunately though, the window, though boarded, had a gap wide enough for her to see through. It was a long, dark, cold vigil. And even when two men did arrive, after a seemingly endless time, they were so muffled as to be quite unrecognizable. Indeed, the only thing Thea thought to have gained from her visit (apart from Georgina's foolish reticule, and the curious fact of Jeremy Tregannan's taking the girl to an obviously secret house) was the vague knowledge of a plot and the witnessing of the ultimate farewells at the gate among the five men. They shook hands, their lips moved formally in turn, in some unheard password presumably, and then, ceremoniously and simultaneously, they rubbed their hands across their brows, the right thumb sticking out like a horn. There was yet one more discovery to come. As they were parting, one of the brethren raised his penetrating voice, to shout at Jeremy, who had already turned his horse, "Nothing to do, then, but wait a sennight! You'll be in touch with us by then, brother!"

Jeremy, turning his nag again, signaled his agreement, but furiously admonished the speaker for his noisy indiscretion, although with little visible effect: the man shrugged, and turned to his fellow traveler. They all seemed tough, independent, and dangerous, these friends, or followers, or whatever they were, Thea reflected, watching the group break up.

At last, she felt they must all be well gone, and it would be safe for her to venture out. Cold and shaking, she descended the stairs, along the very edge, with the same caution she had climbed them, left the house, shut and locked the outer door, hid the heavy key once again deep in the guttering of the eaves, and, thanking God for a patient, well-trained mount (although reflecting all the same that Jeremy's horse and those of the travelers must have taken a route away from where Silver was tethered), collected her mare where she had left her, and rode towards the Bartons', more dead than alive. The wet mist had by now descended thoroughly again, and Thea started at every bush, strained her ears at every harmless country rustling, until even Silver became jumpy and side-stepped home, and rearing once, almost threw her, as a hare crossed their path. But she reached her destination at last and having rubbed Silver down, and given her two lumps of the sugar she always carried in her riding habit, she made her way to bed, Georgina's fateful reticule still swinging from her wrist. Before she fell into an exhausted sleep, she decided she would send an urgent message over as early as possible to Miles next morning, that she must speak to him at once. It would undoubtedly be best to get his advice before approaching anyone else in authority (the more especially as Georgina was at least in some way involved, and between them they might devise some manner of keeping her out of the public eye). For, after all, Thea remembered sleepily, they had, according to the Yorkshire visitors, a sennight before anything should happen. Utterly worn out, she was asleep before she could puzzle out *what* was likely to happen.

Chapter 10

THE next day had a disappointment in store: feeling
very pulled and hagged, Thea nevertheless rose early
and, penning an urgent yet discreet note to Miles Barrett,
suggested she call on him as early that morning as should
not attract comment. (She had thought to suggest his
coming to her, but decided against this, since William
Barton, finding a neighbor abroad at his house at such
an hour, would doubtless conclude the call was for his
benefit; and his presence would be, to say the least, un-
welcome.)

Her own coachman, however, whom she had sent with
strict instructions to hand the note to no one but Miles
himself, returned it with the wafer unbroken, and the information that Miles was away all day, having left the
previous afternoon, and not expected to return until Lord
Bowland's ball that evening. There was nothing to be

done, Thea decided, but possess her soul in patience for the rest of the day, and somehow contrive to speak to Miles privately at the ball itself. It was still too soon to seek out Georgina and return her reticule, so Thea spent an hour or so restlessly tormenting herself with possible alternatives to keeping her startling information to herself till the evening: should she, perhaps, tell William Barton instead, and ask his discretion over Georgina? But then, although kind, he was so full of moral rectitude . . . Finally, having taken herself to task for havering, and firmly decided to wait for Miles's return, she called her carriage and set off, still early, in no very amiable frame of mind to give Georgina back her reticule and, at the same time, some very serious advice.

Georgina, too, looked hagged, her face pale, her hands a–tremble; and one glance at her admired Thea's countenance served only to increase their trembling. Silently, Thea handed her the reticule, saying coldly as she did so,

"You had best examine it carefully, and make sure there is nothing missing. Though I feel you will be glad to hear, the place, when I reached it, was deserted and the bag exactly where you had described it."

Georgina's hands were so unsteady she had difficulty even in untying the cord, but a meticulous examination, under Thea's forbidding eye, revealing that all was as it should be, she managed to collect her wits a little and offer her early guest some hot chocolate. "For I feel sure you will need it, it is so cold today . . . and must have been quite terribly so last night," she added in so small and shaking a voice that Thea relented a little.

But although tolerant of a great deal, of silliness, of temper, of overhigh spirits, even indiscretion, and much else in the very young, Thea could not abide deceitfulness; and this, she felt, was above all what Georgina was guilty of. She therefore said, a little less stiffly, but in tones far different from her usual affectionate ones,

"Now that the question of your reticule is settled, we can discuss, at least to some extent, your conduct. Though, of course, it will be your father who will deal in the main with this on his return . . . I take it you have spoken to *no one*—and I mean to have the truth, Georgina—to *no one*, I say, of this affair?"

Feeling, as she concluded this speech, that Georgina might still, however, slip slyly, as it were, through a lacuna in her query, she elaborated,

"That is to say, that no one at all knows either of your secret meetings with this young man, nor of the meeting place, nor, of course, of the lost reticule?"

"No," replied Georgina, her eyes wide with fear and apprehension.

Thea, looking hard at her, could not, as far as she was able, detect any equivocation or deceit in this reply. She therefore continued, though with rather less hope of a similar denial,

"Does anyone know of your . . . penchant . . . no, I suppose I had better say . . . 'passion' . . . for Mr. Tregannan? And his . . . supposed . . . return of it?"

Georgina flared up at once. "There is no supposition about it! He *does* . . ."

"I did not ask your opinion about his affections, Georgina. Merely whether anyone knows how you feel."

The white anger in Thea's voice, combined with an indefinable touch of contempt, shocked Georgina. She replied, very low,

"No. No one."

"What! Not even Selina and Lucy? Or your personal maid?"

The surprise and cynicism in the cold voice were not lost on Georgina. She answered at once, in all apparent sincerity, "No, I swear it!"

Thea, inwardly contemplating that this seemed out of character as she knew Georgina these days, and uncertain, too, about the girl's maid knowing nothing (for Georgina could hardly be called discreet), was wondering how far to trust this statement, when an explanation of its veracity was given her by Georgina herself, who said, unsteadily,

"Jeremy forbade it, you see. He warned me especially against my abigail, and . . . well, he gave all kinds of good reasons . . . my age, everyone's prejudice, and that kind of thing, against revealing our . . . love . . . to anyone. And he was so . . . definite . . . I, well, I just knew he was right, and so I kept the secret."

Thea's heart smote her a little. She said, far more gently,

"Oh, Georgina, you poor, foolish child! Hasn't your father always been kindness itself since his return? And hasn't everyone loved you, and been kind to you, since you left your Uncle and Aunt? If this had happened during your sojourn with them, it would still be wrong, but more understandable, at least. But why should you so deceive those people who love you? They are not ogres. And they would always have your best interests at heart."

This rebuke, so sadly given, and the new gentleness in

Thea's voice, were too much for Georgina's facile spirit to support: she burst into tears and, flinging herself on her knees beside her friend, continued to weep bitterly.

Thea, still pitying her, yet took advantage of this remorse and distress to say, stroking the young, pretty head,

"I want you to promise me something; it need only be for a short while, until your father returns and can talk to you about your behavior! It is this: will you give me your solemn word to keep out of Jeremy's way, if he should call today? It is unlikely he will come in the evening, anyway, because of Lord Bowland's ball and he will, without doubt, wish to be there," she added, deliberately heartless, knowing Georgina to be too young to attend. "But if he does come, and at *whatever* hour he comes, will you promise not to see or speak with him?"

Georgina said, quickly, "You forget. He is already gone away for two nights."

"Indeed he is not. He returned to the cottage last night. With two men. I already had your reticule but I was forced to hide."

Georgina looked at her in horror.

"So I will have that promise, please," Thea added. "It is the least you can do, after my nightmare effort on your behalf!"

There was a long pause, until Georgina said, slowly, "How can I refuse him if he calls? It will look so . . . so odd."

"Not if you have a bad headache, one that confines you to bed all day. That way, all that is necessary is a pleasant message sent down (if he *should* call on you), that you are indisposed. *Nothing more*, Georgina."

Georgina slowly raised her head to look unwaveringly into Thea's eyes, and asked unexpectedly,

"And if I should give you no such promise?"

"I shall no longer be your friend, child. Ever." The childishness of this phrase rather appalled Thea; but she found it to have its effect on Georgina: the weeping began afresh—copiously—and Georgina promised. Just, she explained between sobs, until her father's return. And at this latter prospect, the tears flowed even faster. Altogether, it was a harrowing interview, and Thea, who never had had any stomach for playing the bully, in however good a cause, felt a great distaste for it and for herself. But all the same, when she left some half an hour later, Georgina was already tucked up in bed looking, (and by now probably feeling, too), as if she had the worst of megrims. And it was obvious, Thea felt, that this time, at least, her promise was one she would keep.

Having, as it were, sealed off one leak of any information to Jeremy Tregannan, Thea set off back to the Bartons' with an easier mind. And, in fact, despite her warning Georgina against seeing Jeremy that night, she at first thought it far more likely, from what she had heard at the derelict cottage, that he would be on his way to the 'Dales' (presumably the Yorkshire ones), than attending Lord Bowland's ball. And this, she felt, would be a great relief, for she would not have to face him as though unaware of his perfidy; and, too, could discuss matters with Miles without arousing the other's suspicion.

But she had no sooner thought herself into this easier frame of mind, than her thoughts circled again like a caged squirrel, and she began to think it likely that the Yorkshiremen's arrival might have caused an alteration in

Jeremy Tregannan's plans, enabling him to postpone his
journey, and so attend tonight's affair, with all the extra
risks his presence would bring . . . She sighed. She had
never felt less like attending a social occasion in her life,
yet she must take care to behave as though all was well
until she could talk with Miles . . . At least, she
concluded with relief, Jeremy had no reason to be suspicious of *her*. And with this thought, she finally wrested her
mind into some kind of repose and managed to act in
her normal, carefree fashion throughout the day. Several
times, however, she found herself shaking a little inwardly
when a horse, or carriage, came up the Bartons' long
drive. Suppose it should be Mr. Tregannan, and she be
forced to be civil and charming to him. But he did not
call and, at last, she was safe in her bedchamber preparing
for the evening's entertainment, and the drive thereto.

Chapter 11

THE ball was a very grand affair indeed and fully as interesting as Thea had anticipated. Aristocracy, county (elegant or eccentric), royalty (in the persons of the two royal brothers), various rich 'Cits' who had married well, the famous, and, to be frank, the demimonde, too, were there. Edmund Kean, small of stature, yet immensely vital, fresh from his recent success at Drury Lane, preened it among the ladies especially; and Lord Byron, still behaving according to Caroline Lamb's description as "Mad, Bad, and Dangerous to Know," languished apart, seemingly overcome with boredom; Beau Brummell, his immense popularity waning a little since his estrangement from the Prince Regent, yet with his wit undiminished, held a small, intelligent court. (Thea had chanced to be present, some years ago, when he had made his deliberate gaffe of "Who's your Fat Friend?" and could still revel, inwardly, at the outrage on Prinny's face.)

Yet, for all this, she could not enjoy herself. Her dance program was full, her popularity undiminished, the spectacular gaslight shone dazzling on her elegant ball gown of jonquil silk, with its high waistline and flounced skirt; and revealed in its unwavering clarity her unblemished beauty. Yet her one concern was to find Miles, and her eyes sought him in vain. He could, in fact, have been anywhere in the crush. She accordingly moved unobtrusively and constantly in search of him, greeting some friends, being hailed by others, pausing for a word here, a wave there, but always obsessed by her search. At one point, she found herself face to face with Jeremy Tregannan and feared that the shock of finding him there, when she had hoped he was far away, must have shown. Moreover, something in his manner, his smooth grace, made her ridiculously nervous: he appeared, in some fashion, smug and *knowing*. Yet, she told herself angrily, this could easily be the effect of an overweening conceit, which he usually kept well-hidden, but which she had for some time suspected and which had finally come to light last night, when he thought himself unobserved by his equals and was dealing with his inferiors. He might have mistaken, for instance, her shocked stare for flattering attention. She was, she told herself firmly, behaving nonsensically. So, hiding her apprehension and personal dislike, she chatted amicably with him also until she could, without offense, move on once more.

Unobtrusively, she strolled from ball room to card rooms, and thence into the gentler glow of candlelight (which she, in truth, preferred), in various anterooms and corridors. A little desperate now, she realized that time was passing, and Miles was still absent or, at least, not to be found. But she had only just reflected on this, when she saw him, far away at the end of a particularly long, wide corridor. She was about to move forward, calling his name, when he turned to speak to someone behind him, at present hidden by the turn in the corridor: it proved to be Jeremy Tregannan himself. Shock kept her silent; she observed the two men apparently on good terms, enter a room off the corridor and, as they moved to shut the door, Jeremy flung his arm, in comradely fashion, round his companion's shoulders. When she had gathered her wits again, she descended to the ballroom, and having made her excuses to those gentlemen whose dances she had missed ("a torn flounce, so tiresome, but I'm sure you will forgive me"), determinedly entered into the spirit of the ball while, at the same time, keeping her eyes open for the return of either, or both, men.

At one point in the evening, just before supper, she was seated for a brief moment deliberately hidden in an alcove, attempting to recover her breath and reflecting that Miles and Jeremy had been gone for at least a good hour, when she heard, behind her chair, the pleasant tones of the Beau.

"Ah, Miss Langham, I see you seek peace and quiet too! It is some time since we have met, is it not?" And then, mischievously, "I fear I no longer frequent quite *all* the polite circles as you yourself continue to do!"

Thea turned at once, a pleased smile on her lips; she had long liked the Beau and was aware of his confidential remark made to Lady Hester Stanhope that if people were so foolish as to follow his every whim, why should he not play up to them. What, as he put it, did it signify?

"You have been sadly missed, I assure you, sir. Life has been less—colorful—with your absence!"

"But my presence would not make it *gaudy,* I hope, ma'am?" he teased, as, indeed, she hoped he would, knowing his dislike of loud vulgar colors, her reason for making so provoking a remark. All the same, she reflected unhappily, he did not look as he had a year ago. There was something sad about him, not weary, as some would have it, but somber, as though his love of life had somehow deserted him. He was said, she knew, to be in some financial straits, too; but that should not worry him, for there were many intelligent and moneyed people who were very fond of him still and thought little of the Regent for dropping him so spitefully. But, of course, he was said to be very proud . . . She became aware of having remained silent a little too long and, simultaneously, of Beau Brummell himself looking at her as consideringly as she, inwardly at least, had been contemplating him. He said, slowly,

"You have always had my respect and admiration, Miss Langham, not only for your . . . elegance . . . both of mind and looks, but for your kindly understanding." She glanced up at him, astonishment in her fine eyes, and he went on, a curious, rueful amusement on his face,

"You must not worry about me, you know, and imagine my . . . my *star* to be in a decline! I am, I assure you, perfectly content, and, indeed, happier now that I am beginning to know my true friends from my time-servers and fools!"

Thea, in some confusion, unable for once to dissimulate

politely, could only ask, "Are my thoughts, then, so transparent?"

"No, of course not! Not as a rule . . . but I suspect that tonight, anyway, you have something on your own mind that brings you no happiness . . . And you are, accordingly, not your usual composed self. If I can be of service. . . ?"

"You are remarkably astute, sir, and I thank you. But that is my misfortune—I can confide in no one at present!"

He remained looking down at her, with the same gentle smile on his face. "I will not bother you further with your misfortune then. Let me try to divert you by thanking you for the compliment of calling me 'astute'."

Thea laughed. "I have long known you to be so, sir—and so have many others."

"Ah, we are neither of us fools, you and I. Although I must admit to behaving like one for more than a decade of my life." He paused again, but Thea kept silent, certain he would speak further, and intrigued to know what he would have to say. He continued at last,

"Have you never wondered at my utter obsession with fashion, which cannot but be ridiculous to all men of sense?"

"Why, sir, I am aware of your remarks to Lady Hester. And apart from that, it is you who have changed men from gaudy popinjays to reasonably clothed, dignified males. That surely, is not a ridiculous obsession, but rather a gift to humanity." Thea kept her voice light, in keeping with his yet, beneath the casual elegance, she was convinced there was a serious purpose. And she was not mistaken, for her companion went on, unsmiling now,

"You know, my . . . beginnings were, shall we say,

obscure. My grandfather was a personal servant, and my father a small government clerk who, to my eternal gratitude, bettered himself and got me, somehow, to Eton. But all the same, I saw something of the seamy side of life, and that at an age not too young to understand . . . I must tell you, ma'am, I did my utmost to avoid it as swiftly as I could. And I succeeded, as you will admit, beyond my wildest dreams . . . But it left me with a kind of, of what our Prussian allies call *angst*—lethargy, world weariness—call it what you like! I could do nothing to alleviate that sordid past (for I am not, I freely admit, the stuff reformers or saints are made of), but the uselessness of many of our lives . . . the wild pursuits of trivia . . . I suppose this encouraged me to worship fashion . . . After all," he added, with rather more of his usual insouciance, "it is as good a piece of trivia as anything else!"

"I think, perhaps, you rather despise the Society that took you up, many of whom still worship you, sir!"

"Oh, that is coming it a little too strong, ma'am. *Individuals*, I sincerely like—you, if I may say so without offense, among them. But others . . . Do you know, I think I have a sly, black humor, that takes it out on idle fools, inspiring them to the most ridiculous lengths of fashion, gulling them with outrageous statements about laundering my linen and such like . . . and I have *enjoyed* it," he added, with obvious surprise, as though the thought had just occurred to him, "perhaps because in my young days, unlimited fresh linen was far from easy to come by!"

Thea, who had heard from her cousins many stories of the Beau and his wasted cravats, for instance, laughed and admitted to believing him and, moreover, sympathizing with him.

"But in the end," he replied, "I went too far . . . my remark to Alvaney was deliberate social suicide. And yet, at the time, I enjoyed that, too!"

Thea, remarking the past tense, would not ask him if he now regretted his insult to his royal former friend and patron. At that moment a group of people approached them, and their quiet tête-à-tête was broken. The Beau turned to her with a flourish, and paying her some witty and extravagant compliment, moved away. Only the deep respect and the sadness in his eyes, revealed to her alone, betrayed him. She smiled and waved farewell. It was the last time she ever spoke to him: within less than two years, he was fled to France, in debt and disgraced.

To Thea's relief, Miles was among the approaching party and, better still, she could see no sign of Jeremy. She moved forward at once to speak with him. As she came nearer, she discerned some suppressed fury, some deep inner disturbance in his expression. She contrived to separate him a little from the group and to say, discreetly, "Miles, I must speak with you at once." But he looked at her so vaguely, as though his thoughts were elsewhere, or turned inward, that she felt compelled to add, "It concerns Mr. Tregannan, and it cannot wait."

At the mention of this name, Miles's eyes focused at once, their clearness curiously reddened to utter fury, and he responded to her startled gaze by saying, through his teeth,

"Then I'll wager it's no good you have to tell me. Come."

Ignoring some innocent guest about to approach them,

he turned on his heel, and with Thea close behind, led the way from the ballroom to a small study, quite isolated but close by, for he was an old friend of Lord Bowland's and knew the house well. Thea, preceding him through the door, which he closed immediately and firmly behind him, reflected it was as well that it was the hour for supper, and most guests were so occupied with finding places, or dancing attendance on womenfolk, that his curt manner had been remarked hardly at all; only, perhaps, by the recent guest left standing solitary at their abrupt departure. And he was, hopefully, of little consequence.

Chapter 12

THEA'S one thought, naturally, was of Georgina, and seeing the red fury still in Miles's eyes as he placed a chair for her, then himself stood before the fireplace, she felt suddenly faint. She overcame the momentary weakness, however, and was forming in her mind how best to speak when, before she could do so, Miles said abruptly,

"That damned blackguard! He met me this evening, almost upon my arrival here, and with hardly time for me to apologize to my host for an unavoidable lateness . . . He said, with great friendliness, that he had at last recalled that I was correct, and that we had indeed seen each other before he came to Yew Tree Mansion and that he knew I should be interested to discover where." Miles stopped as suddenly as he had started and then went on, somewhat more calmly.

"Well, as you know, I have never much liked the

fellow; and tonight I was certainly as disposed to discover where I had seen him, as *he* was to be friendly . . . So at his suggestion we turned away from the ballroom and card tables and found a quiet place to talk."

"I saw you," said Thea, very low. "But you both seemed so . . . amicable, as well as preoccupied, that I went away again."

"You were searching for me?" He sounded surprised.

"Yes. I . . ." Thea, thinking quickly, decided it would be best to hear Miles's story first, since it could well explain a great deal. She therefore said, with as much ease as she could muster,

"But my tale can wait: I think yours may well be the more important!"

At first, he seemed disposed to argue. Then his mood changing suddenly, he asked solicitously, "Are you sure, my dear? You look so . . . so peaked and chilled!" But when Thea waved away his concern impatiently, he contented himself with insisting on drawing her chair nearer the fire and continued, bitterly,

"He knows about Annabel, my little cyprian. He was in Paris, in the same arrondissement at the time, and observed me often. And so, too, must I have seen him, but without realizing it . . ." Miles paused, a grim look on his face, and then went on, slowly this time,

"Do you know . . . I felt from the first that his sudden meeting me this evening—and with such friendliness —was a cover for *something;* although *what,* I could not make out. Indeed, I was at first prepared for some approach . . . an appeal for a personal loan, perhaps, or some such thing. But then, instead, he continued to talk of the poverty of that Paris quarter, the filth, the dirt, the hopelessness, the unspeakable distress, and I found myself in complete agreement with him, saying, indeed, that no country, no government, should permit its poor and needy to degenerate to such a state." He glanced down into Thea's now apprehensive eyes and went on, a harder tone creeping into his voice,

"I will be brief, and not bore you with the circumlocutions, the hints, the gradual edging through to the final point, but what his conversation ultimately came to was this, that he knew of what he called my sympathies with the downtrodden, the oppressed, and the poverty-stricken; that my demeanor in France, and every word spoken this evening, and on other occasions too, revealed it. And that he was therefore—'making so bold' was his expression— as to enlist my 'active help' for the Luddite cause . . ."

"The *Luddites?* But apart from rare occasions, they are quiet—or long gone—from this part of the world . . ."

"They are not *visible,* Thea, which is a different thing. But *are* still very active, as you know, in Yorkshire and in Derbyshire and Nottinghamshire, too. Anyway, for the moment that is beside the point . . . I told him to his face that I was no revolutionary but a loyal subject of King George the Third, and that he had best speak to me no more of the matter since I would have none of it. I added that, this one time, between gentlemen, I would forget the conversation had taken place—unless anything untoward happened—when I should remember it quickly enough."

"It was then he threatened you?" asked Thea, thinking of Georgina; of the secret meeting, with Jeremy as its leader, in the discreetly hidden house; and of the mention of the 'sennight of quiet,' before, presumably, a storm.

"Yes. He said he hoped my idealism would have been sufficient to insure my support. But if it would not, then he would spread the word about my 'long liaison' with Annabel." Miles snorted. "I told him to spread what he liked, and be damned. And that if it came to *that,* I should instantly initiate inquiries myself, and put the constables on to him for his manner of speaking with me this night!"

Thea, with sinking heart, went on,

"So he threatened you with something—*someone*—else?"

"Yes . . ." To Thea's consternation, Miles suddenly put his face in his hands. "He says Georgina is hopelessly compromised . . ."

At this Thea cried instinctively, "But that is not true, Miles! I feel sure of it. I must tell you I discovered yesterday that she . . ."

"He swears she is *enceinte* by him, Thea. Over two months."

Thea looked up in horror. Surely Georgina had not lied so utterly to her? She remembered the unsteady voice, the excess of tears, the violence of the girl's emotion . . . and unbidden, the words '*usually* we kiss and hold hands' rose to her mind. She went on in a low voice. "Perhaps things may not be as dreadful as they seem. He may be . . . exaggerating. But frankly I am now not sure . . . Before I give you my story—which, alas, has some considerable bearing on the situation—tell me, what did Mr. Tregannan actually want you to do? I mean, in support of the Luddite cause?"

"He wished a vast sum of money, to start with. I should guess he is in need of a large sum—perhaps as a bribe— at once, by his manner. Anyway, as you must know, there are spies everywhere, and agents provocateurs, and double-dealers even within the minor ranks of government authority in the counties most concerned with the Luddite cause; and keeping some steadfast for that cause, and bribing others to it, must require a great deal of what he called in the vernacular, 'the blunt' . . ."

There was a long pause. Then Miles spoke again. "I confess, I cannot find it in my heart to condemn those men who support the Luddites through devotion alone, or idealism—or even desperation (and I am persuaded many of *these* would otherwise be as loyal as you or I). Above all, the simple souls . . . hungry, desperate for their families . . . even believing in King Lud in his Sherwood Forest, perhaps—they are to be pitied and helped . . . but *legally* . . . Yet for each one of these simple idealists there are others—not Luddites at all, but jackals, who meddle for money; or vicious rowdies, who commit arson and murder for mere sport—many, many of them. And the Jacks, too, Jacobins, crazed men, with an alien cause at heart! Or other still active revolutionaries . . . the Paineities . . . all are involved." He added, spacing his words and beating his fist impotently on the mantel, "And even for my daughter, I will not help them!"

Thea asked, thinking mostly to divert his thoughts, "And did you say as much to Mr. Tregannan?"

"I did. I also taunted him—quite deliberately, to provoke some kind of revelation from him, I admit—with being a rogue, out to exploit, for self-interest . . ." Miles paused and then, looking directly into Thea's face, said earnestly,

"He is not. He is a fanatic. Exactly for what cause I

do not know. Only that he is not to be bought. Indeed, he replied, quite dispassionately, that he was, as he put it, 'dedicated'; but whether for political ends, or for a personal ideal, he would not say, since, he explained, he 'would give me no aid to uncover his activities.' But that therefore, to him, the end justified both the means and the instruments . . . He is dangerous, Thea—of that I am convinced."

"He *may* be an earnest Luddite or, as we originally suspected, a Frenchman. A republican with the rabid ideas of some French still, on the subject . . . And none too happy, therefore," Thea continued thoughtfully, "with the return to Imperialism, and now Monarchy, in his own land."

"So he must make trouble here! It is possible, I suppose, but I think Luddism the more likely, unless he is even more devious than we imagine. For I have not told you the half of what he demands of me: he needs, he says, a 'well-born' spy; an agent placed higher than any of the 'dedicated Luddites,' who are mostly simple men. One who can discover—through friends in high government places, for instance—the government's planned countermeasures to any uprisings, especially those on a large scale; so that such measures can be rendered ineffectual. One who can identify government traitors who have penetrated Luddite groups. One to interfere and upset government policies generally, in fact."

Thea gazed at him in horror. She said, faintly, knowing her protest to be foolish, "But they—the Luddites at least—*have* their supporters in high places. Lord Byron spoke up for them in the House even, and many Whig gentlemen . . ."

"These are honorable men, Thea!" Miles added with a quirk of his eyebrow and more like his old self. "Even Lord Byron—politically—and loyal ones. They would no more dream of defiling that honor by spying and such, than of touching pitch . . . What Tregannan wants is a *dishonorable* man, who appears as upright as those you have just mentioned. He hopes to have one in *me*. He does not care how that man has become dishonorable, as long as he does his bidding."

"You *cannot*. Why, if the Jacobins are involved as well as the Luddites, to say nothing of other French influences . . ."

"No, of course, I cannot," answered Miles, irritably. "And I told him so! He has misjudged me, first as an idealist as rabid as himself, then as a rogue—the latter, I suspect, because he was not fully cognizant of the reason for my long stay in France with Annabel, or my lies on my return . . . But the question is, what am I to do? My poor Georgina . . ." He began to pace up and down in considerable distress, and went on, somewhat confusedly, seemingly at a tangent,

"I said I suspected, as he had been so long in the district, he had a mind to stir up trouble in Lancashire, and possibly elsewhere, and needed, at least to some extent, my money to accomplish this . . ." Again Miles paused, then continued, through his teeth, "And I added that in such a case it gave me additional pleasure to refuse him . . . and made the sacrifice of my daughter (if, indeed, matters were as he implied) less hard."

Thea could say nothing, only wait for that agonized voice to continue,

"As I said earlier, I think by his reaction I hit the mark,

that he needs the money, and urgently, for he turned white and looked, for the moment, crazed as though he would fly at me. But then all he *said,* quite calmly, was that if I failed him he would have to try other sources; he had asked me first since he had expected, because of my compassion for the poverty-stricken, for those unable to help themselves, my burning sense of justice, to find me more sympathetic to his cause . . ." Miles buried his face in his hands.

"And at this, I fear, I shouted, 'To find me more sympathetic? Aye! By compromising my daughter, making her an object of derision to the world!' Do you know, he smiled, and said something like, 'Ah, no. If you had obliged me with the sum I asked for, and agreed, even in part, to my suggestions, I would rather have sought Georgina's hand in marriage, than blazon abroad the fact that she is to have a child. Even to *you.* . . .' Oh God! I fear it is true about Georgina, my dear Thea."

Thea, lost in pity, now felt inclined to agree. And yet . . . She did not reply directly, therefore, but asked instead,

"And what if you had refused to allow her to marry him?"

"He would doubtless have forced my hand by revealing her condition . . . just, indeed, as he is doing now. But I think he imagined it would not come to such a pass: he had the insolence to point out that it was well-known I could refuse Georgina nothing and . . . and that as she was certainly wild for him, and he chanced to be 'quite fond,' as he put it, of her, all would have been well . . . That there are many such marriages."

Miles turned away, his head bowed. "That is really all

there is to tell, my dear Thea: except that he added that if Georgina's condition becomes known, her future will be ruined, and it will be I who made it so, not he . . . He has given me five days in which to change my mind and aid him."

Thea, unable to look on at such misery, said staunchly, "I still feel he may be bluffing, on this point at least! Anyway, how does he propose to make the matter public (if you refuse to comply with his requests) without endangering his own affairs?"

Miles's laugh seemed almost genuine. "Oh, by a discreet word here, a whisper there—social gatherings are notorious listening posts, are they not? He even mentioned scurrilous broadsheets!" Miles's face set. "As he pointed out, it would soon be the *on-dit* of Society, and whether Georgina remained for a little to face things out or went hastily into retreat, either way she would give herself away." (He did not add Jeremy's brutal remark that Georgina was 'thickening fast.') But he thought bitterly of it, so that he hardly heard Thea saying,

"And you, you would then declare his plot. So *he* would have lost, too!"

"*What* plot, Thea? I might more likely be taken for a furious and therefore crazed parent. We have *nothing,* my dear, to go on. And nothing treasonable, or even illegal, to associate him with!"

"But we have," Thea broke in triumphantly, "*something,* at least! Listen!" She thought it best to mention first, albeit somewhat uncertainly now, Georgina's perhaps specious denials of any degree of intimacy between herself and Jeremy; and then began her account of the previous evening's occurrences. But she found herself to be shivering violently as she recalled the house and the long, terrifying vigil, and struggling to control herself, was surprised to find Miles's arms about her, arranging a scarfshawl he had discovered on a nearby stool, and chafing her cold hands with his own.

It came to her, suddenly, how willingly she could lean against him, and compel his arms to remain about her, if the time were not so desperate . . . Struggling to control so ridiculous a weakness, however, she finished her story. There was a long, contemplative silence, until Miles rose, and walking over to the windows, drew aside the curtains to stare out into the night,

"You say you understood a week is to pass before anything further happens . . . What, and where, I wonder . . . here, in Lancashire after all this time? And is the delay caused by some particular lack of funds, as I suspect, and is Jeremy's sudden approach to me the result of this? Or is it pure chance that two came so closely?" He released the curtain and moved abruptly as the little French ormolu clock on the mantel chimed delicately yet another hour. "We can do no more tonight. And unless we appear soon you will be looked at askance by the company, or, far worse, with suspicion by Jeremy, who may guess I have talked to you, as a friend of Georgina's . . . Come, my dear, we cannot have you endangered," he put out his hand, "we shall reappear circumspectly and separately. And tonight, as soon as I can safely leave this place," his voice was harsh, "I shall speak with Georgina."

"You . . . you will tell me what . . . what . . ."

"Of course, my dear Thea. I thank God it was *you* Georgina turned to!"

He paused by the door, adding slowly,

"I think we had best continue outwardly as though nothing had happened. After I have seen Georgina tonight, I must work out how best to handle matters so that we can at least gain a little more information regarding this seeming plot you have told me of, in the few days available. I think our households have a visit to Pendle Hill arranged for tomorrow. Is that not so?"

Thea nodded.

"Well, I shall contrive to talk to you there, my dear . . . of Georgina and of any ideas I may have had. Come, you must not look so wan. I shall go before you into the ballroom and shall expect soon to glimpse you from a distance as radiant as ever!"

With a sudden movement he kissed her fingers, one by one, with a gentleness so different from his last bitter, cold remarks that Thea caught her breath. She was left, her hands now clasped, thinking confusedly that although she was familiar with this gesture from other times and other men, she had never before felt quite as she did now.

Chapter 13

*T*HE *following day was, unfortunately for Thea's peace* of mind, at least, wet and windy, far from the usual fine, open weather both households had looked for when they had sometime previously arranged the picnic to Pendle Hill. The expedition was consequently cancelled, Miles Barrett sending a servant over quickly to suggest this, and the Bartons fully concurring, adding that both families had best stay in their own homes. Thea, needless to say, had more than an inkling that other, far weightier matters than damp and depressing weather had caused Miles's urgent message of cancellation, and wondered constantly, with great anxiety, whether Jeremy Tregannan's statement about Georgina's delicate state were true or not, and if Miles Barrett had, either way, come to any conclusion about how best to deal with the man and his threats.

133

In the end, she could bear neither her own company, nor that of the others, feeling cooped up in the Bartons' mansion, vast though it was. Soon after a light nuncheon had been served, William retired to his study, the girls went off somewhere about their own devices, and Thea and her hostess repaired to Maria's boudoir, which was in the old part of the house. It was small, panelled, and charming, and as a bride she had refused to allow her William to alter one stone of it, or any part of the tiny knot garden outside. Shortly, however, Thea rose to her feet and announced her intention of having Silver saddled up and going for a canter.

Maria looked up aghast. "Thea, you must have run mad! You will catch your death of cold, and besides, be soaked to the skin before you are even beyond the home park!"

Thus addressed, Thea strolled nonchalantly to the window, intending to remark that a little rain hurt no one, and she was not, anyway, made of icing sugar like some of her sex. But a closer look at the weather through the ancient leaded panes revealed rain slashing down like rapiers. There was nothing for it, Thea reflected, she would have to remain indoors, locked in with her secret worries. If only she could have discussed the matter with someone—Maria perhaps, for she was sensible enough, in all conscience. But she had promised to speak to no one. If only Miles were *here* . . . .

Maria, seeing her friend's brooding expression, naturally mistook it for disappointment and boredom, and though a little surprised—for Thea was never childish or moody—suggested diffidently that if Thea felt she really must go out, would she not do better to take the big old traveling coach. The roads, if she did not go too far or stray off the main highway, would be perfectly satisfactory, there was a curious kind of covered box for the driver (invented by William's eccentric father, who had had a fondness for his very elderly chief coachman), and she felt quite sure that Barney, his younger successor, would not object, probably being as bored as Thea by this terrible weather.

Thea doubted this, for her quick eye had already observed Barney to be head over ears for one of the young, pretty maids engaged about the place. All the same she gladly took up the offer of the coach, but only if the rain should abate a little, and then with Thomas, her own man, at the reins.

"I am not such a monster as to give servants, or horses, for that matter, a soaking for a mere whim, my dear," she laughed, "and I can do very well at home—really. I have innumerable letters to write . . . All the same, if the weather clears a little, I *will* go, if you will excuse me, just for a brief excursion. And, as I have already decided, with my own man Thomas, who will certainly put me to rights if I ask too much of him, since he has known me from my infancy!"

Thus it came about that an hour later, when the rain became less violent, she was preparing to leave and had even furnished herself, or rather her conscience, with an excuse—the purchase of thread for Maria's embroidery —in a certain shop away down in the market town.

"You will not wish me to come with you?" Maria asked doubtfully.

"No, my dear. You are kindness itself; but no! I cannot think what has come over me—" (a white lie, that!) "and I promise to come back no longer glum."

Thomas, her own coachman, well wrapped in oil skins, and with the horses well covered too—'just in case' as he put it—was waiting outside for her, one bristly eyebrow cocked.

"Ye'll never grow up, Missie, will you? Gallivanting around the countryside on such a day as this!"

"You don't mind, Thomas? The truth is I . . . I have a megrim, and only fresh air will cure it."

"Well, drop your window the wee—est quarter of an inch, and ye'll get plenty of *that*, I'm thinking! But no," he added in a kindly voice, "*I* don't mind, I'd rather be out and about myself. And don't fret yourself about the horses, *they'll* be fine! So where are we off to then, Miss Thea?"

It crossed Thea's mind to change her direction and drive over to Miles's, but she decided this to be officious and far too distant since the normal route by the ford would now almost certainly be impassable. Anyway, she would be of little help to Miles, for, after all, he would have ridden or sent over if he had needed her assistance. Hence she repeated her request to be taken to the silks shop first; and afterwards, supposing the weather to have improved still more, to the rather superior milliner's to buy some quilled lace she had in mind for the sewing woman to put on one of her gowns. With a pleasant nod of comprehension, Thomas flicked his whip, and they rumbled off.

Everything wilted and dripped. The hedgerows drooped and glistened, the trees swayed dismally, the late roses round one of the cottages in the village wept, the sky swung leaden and sad above them. It was hardly a way to lighten her spirits and yet, all the same, it was a relief to be on the move. She alighted at the small shop in the main street where Maria always bought her embroidery thread and, the rain having suddenly stopped and the wind died down a little, she considerately told Thomas he could rest up the horses in the main Coaching Inn, and take a little time off himself.

"I shall probably take a stroll myself, at least as far as the milliner's, and will be ready to leave from the main Inn within one hour precisely. Unless," Thea added, "the weather worsens again. In that case I shall repair to the Inn at once, and expect the horses to be harnessed quickly, ready to leave."

This having been arranged, they parted company. Thea, having selected Maria's silks in a leisurely manner, and purchased some fine cambric herself, to edge handkerchiefs (which she knew, in her heart, her natural restlessness would never let her complete), then walked on down to the dark little shop where she had, on Maria's recommendation, decided to search for her lace. One side of the shop looked out onto a narrow street, and she was seated in the window on this side, mildly studying a rather astonishing variety of trimmings (considering that she was so far from London) when, glancing up, she noted that she was almost opposite one of the town's taverns. There was her own coachman, Thomas, leaning against the door, in amicable if somewhat rowdy conversation with several men, one or two of whom were obviously friends of his. Nothing was remarkable in the scene, and normally Thea would not have spared it a second glance, but something in the stance of one of the group caught her eye, and, the shop window being open, (the atmosphere in the small room having become damp and steamy from wet hems

and rain-soaked garments, where it mingled with the heat
from an oil lamp already lit since the day was so dark),
she heard, in a sudden chance silence, the soft, strange
Lancashire-Irish voice from the deserted house.

The samples sank forgotten into her lap, and drawing
her chair a little to one side, so as not to be observed, she
gave her whole attention to the group opposite, straining
her ears to hear further. From the little she could hear,
however, the conversation was, without doubt, harmless:
the Irishman named, or nicknamed as she remembered,
Mick, was telling an amusing story, and all were undoubtedly enjoying it. But gradually a few other loafers strolled
over to the group, and as they did so, Thea chanced to see
the same knuckle-on-forehead signal pass unobtrusively
between one of the newcomers and one of the men who
had originally lounged alongside Thomas. This gesture,
she began to notice, occurred several times between different members of the group, and now there was a general
move to enter the tavern by a side door, instead of loung-
ing outside. Thomas followed with the rest, but whether
aware of any underlying motive or conspiracy, Thea was
quite unable to judge.

Nor was she to have any chance to find out, for even as
Thomas was wandering amiably inside, talking busily at
the same time, he glanced up at the sky, and scowled.
Thea, looking up likewise, saw the clouds lowering once
more (she had, in fact, been too immersed in the scene
before her to take much heed of the steadily darkening
sky). Already scattered drops began to fall. Her coachman
at once backed out of the tavern entrance shouting farewells and began running heavily toward the Inn where the
horses had been stabled. Thea likewise, putting up her

elegant but rather flimsy umbrella, hastened in the same direction, fortunately not much more than a stone's throw away. By the time she arrived, Thomas already had the coach backed out, and she sank gratefully against the squabs, her few parcels scattered around her.

On the journey home, wet and windy once more, Thea debated within herself whether to ask Thomas if he knew of any conspiracy, or of the identities of the men who had so carefully and surreptitiously exchanged signals. With her natural delicacy, she felt any such question to be an invasion of his private life and world; even more so if, (as was quite likely since as well as being a Southerner, he was a solid and loyal servant), he were unaware of anything untoward. Finally, however, the possible seriousness of the situation outweighed all other considerations; she reminded herself that he had stood her friend since she was in leading strings, helped her onto her first pony, taught her innumerable skills of horsemanship as the years passed, including how to manage a four-in-hand; and, the rain having once again stopped (indeed it was more like April than late summer), she took a deep breath and knocking on the panel asked him to stop the coach a minute and confer with her.

Mystified, Thomas climbed down from the box and, standing by the open window, his hard, flat beaver off, asked her rather abruptly what she required. Thea, for her part, approached the question circumspectly. She explained at first that she had chanced to glimpse him and his friends from the milliner's window and was intrigued, since she had not known him to have so many cronies in this part of the world.

Scratching his head—it was surely, his gesture implied,

an odd time to broach such a subject, in the middle of nowhere and with the heavens about to open again— Thomas explained that, as she well knew, he had been up in these parts with both the master and herself several times before; and the people, while difficult to get to know, once known, remained staunch friends forever.

"Some of those there today, you see, Missie, they's friends of men in Lord Barton's service, for instance, so naturally I knows them too, now."

Thea's hazel eyes and Thomas's comfortable brown ones looked steadily at each other.

"And do you know the Irishman? Well, he's north-country, but he's still got his underlying brogue. An amusing fellow, to all appearances."

There was a pause. Their gaze remained steady, until Thomas answered slowly, seemingly reluctantly, "I . . . I knows him a little, Miss Thea, but he's no close friend, if that's what you're asking."

"Do you . . . trust . . . these men, Thomas? Believe me, I have good *reason* for asking."

"Ah, now, Miss Thea, that's a strange question. They're honest men. I trust them not to rob, say."

It was now quite obvious to Thea that her coachman was hedging; with the bluntness of long acquaintance and respect, she therefore said, outright,

"Thomas, I speak in confidence . . . but I know, and I think *you* know, that among that group of people today there were men who . . . who conspire against the . . . the peace of the realm."

"Not among *my* friends, that there are *not*, ma'am!" The reply was instant and uncompromising.

Thea smiled her habitual, sweet smile. "I am sure of

that, Thomas. I have no doubt of your loyalty to . . .
well, in fact to your King, as well as to my father. But
. . . they were not *all* friends of yours at the tavern today
—you have said so yourself already—and among those
people there were enemies of our country, our ordered
realm. Am I not right?"

Thomas looked at her sadly. "That depends, ma'am.
What is an enemy of our country? If our country has a
government that takes bread out of poor men's mouths
with its laws, or. . ." he fumbled a little with his explanation, being, usually, a man of few words, "or allows their
masters to . . . to use machines instead of *paying* men
—well, perhaps it's our country that's wrong, and those
men are right to resent it." He added humbly, "I'm sorry,
Miss Thea, to be so contradictory."

Thea cut him short with a wave of her hand, saying as
she did so, and in some horror, "You wouldn't *help* such
men, though, would you? Believe me, I understand your
feelings, and agree, to some extent, with what you are
saying. But these men are violent!"

"I surely wouldn't help. . . But I wouldn't hinder,
neither, Miss Thea. It's not *my* fight. I want nothing of it.
And masters like your father, or Mr. Barrett, or Lord
Barton—or most of our squires and many landowners,
in fact—have nothing to fear. . ." He added, then, in a
low, half-ashamed voice, that there were, all the same,
others, "these here Lancashire cotton mill owners, and
the Yorkshire wool merchants," for whom nothing favor-
able could be said. They'd downtrod the cotton-spinners,
or their weavers and such like. And if they got their come-
uppance, they'd only themselves to blame.

Thea, wondering a little wildly how she could speak to

Thomas of the much wider repercussions the men were, possibly unwittingly, involving themselves in, was suddenly conscious of the rain falling once again and bouncing off poor Thomas's bare head. She said, hastily, "Well, we can't talk more now, in the middle of a wet field, almost. Up you go; and hurry us home . . . But please, please promise me you . . . you won't do anything until we have spoken again?"

"Bless your heart, missie, I won't *do* anything, anyway! But I'll give you my promise, all the same, if it makes your mind more easy!" And reflecting that his mistress was definitely overset, almost to the point of being unhinged, and far from her usual blithe, balanced self, he did as he was bid, whipping up the horses with a will.

Seated inside the carriage, all Thea could think was that Thomas had spoken to her with all the superior adult kindness he had used when she was a little girl, and obviously took no serious heed of her fears or warnings, thinking her hysterical. Half amused, half angry, half frantic with worry, (for within seven days probably, somehow, somewhere nearby, something was coming to a head —of that she was convinced), she sat stiffly, her thoughts whirling from Georgina, to Jeremy, to the Luddites, and worse. She hoped with all her heart that Miles would be at Lord Barton's on her return. She could at least tell him her further discoveries, and perhaps, between them, they could work out some means of preventing a tragedy. Reflecting that today she had behaved rather like a spy herself, and an hysterical one at that, she smiled wryly, and brought all her considerable strength of character to bear upon considering other more mundane matters. She was only partially successful.

Chapter 14

THEA was fortunate, on returning to Lord Barton's (and being helped down the coach steps very kindly and solicitously by Thomas, as though, she thought with sudden amusement, she were soon destined for Bedlam), to find Miles Barrett, apparently imperturbably and comfortably esconced with the family in the small drawing room. She was less pleased to discover Jeremy Tregannan there also; and manners being so civilized as they were these days, no one would have been aware of any tension or dislike between the two men. Certainly not Lord Barton, who was happily boring his wife and the others, Selina and Lucy included, with a long, rambling account of a new system of crop rotation he was resolved to try.

Feeling out of patience at this too civil behavior, though knowing herself to be unreasonably so, Thea gratefully accepted a dish of tea from Lucy's hands; and deliberately inquiring about Georgina's whereabouts (for she was, thankfully, nowhere to be seen), was informed by Lucy that her friend was confined to bed with a bad chill. Thea dared not, at that moment, look at Miles, but an instant later, the conversation having passed to some other easy subject, she risked a glance in his direction, Jeremy being momentarily occupied with arranging Maria's light shawl for her. She was met by a dark look from Miles's deep blue eyes and realized, intuitively, that he was as anxious to speak privately with her as she with him; though how this was to be accomplished in the circumstances, without arousing the suspicion of one and the surprise of the rest of the party, she had no idea.

As it happened, however, matters fell out well for her. Lord Barton carried Jeremy Tregannan off (willy-nilly, it seemed to Thea, who observed with amusement that gentleman's tactful but unsuccessful attempt to avoid leaving the drawing room party) to see his latest acquisition among his hunters. Lucy and Selina were sent by their eldest sister on some small errand to collect another, warmer wrap and her embroidery from her private sitting room. At this Thea, taking Maria's hand in her own (still cold from the drive), said anxiously and shyly, that if Maria would not mind, she herself wished to speak privately with Miles. Maria, good-natured as ever, feeling the frozen hands, opining that Thea must be sickening for a chill herself, and secretly hoping for a romantic attachment between her dear friend and Mr. Barrett, said pleasantly that she would willingly take herself off and waylay the girls too. She then gave Thea a quick kiss and departed, with what could only be called an unsuitably roguish glance (for she often wished Thea as happily married as herself and had sometimes thought to see a fervent gleam in Miles's eyes).

Neither of the two remaining in the room spared a moment to comment in any way on poor Maria's mistaken assumptions. At once Thea asked anxiously,

"Georgina?"

"Tregannan spoke the truth, I fear. Although she assures me it occurred once only."

Thea's face softened. She said, very low, "Oh, poor, poor child! And poor Miles!"

Her gentleness was too much for Miles Barrett who, seeing the beautiful eyes, the now gentle face framed with its halo of bright hair, and suddenly aware of Thea's whole stance of sympathy, first turned abruptly away, and then, almost in the same moment, moved again to put his head down on her shoulder, saying unevenly,

"Oh God, I have been such a bad father! If I had only looked after her better after Jane's death—never gone away—all my selfish peccadilloes—my appalling example!"

"You mustn't reproach yourself; indeed, you must *not*. Since your return no one, *no one*, Miles, could have been a kinder, more sensible or sensitive parent."

He controlled his distress fiercely and, lifting his head, said dryly that the harm had been done long ago, with his recklessness after his wife's death, and only made worse by his protracted absence later. He then turned to hold Thea's hands very tight, as though for comfort, and went on, in more normal tones, that from Thea's earlier look she had something of moment to impart to him; and that as he was at his wits' end what to do about *enceinte* daughters, Luddites, Jeremy Tregannan, or traitors generally, he would do best, perhaps, to listen to what she had to say. "Unless I mistake the matter, and you merely wished to hear about Georgina?"

"No, indeed *not*, Miles. I have at least *some* news, and perhaps between us and with Thomas—my coachman, you know—his help, or at least his goodwill, we can avert, to some degree anyway, a tragic occurrence."

At the mention of her coachman, Miles's eyebrows went up, but he made no comment, remaining silent until Thea had told him in full of her experiences that day, including her less than satisfactory talk with Thomas on the journey home. When she had concluded, hastily, for both realized they might at any minute be interrupted, Miles said slowly,

"As you know, I have until the end of the week to 'make up my mind,' as our mysterious and unpleasant Mr. Tregannan puts it, about poor Georgina, and about handing over the sum of money he demands. We spoke briefly again this morning and this time I deliberately led him on. He seems so *urgent* about the money . . . if we can at least discover whether the sum is essential to a particular plan, and perhaps, if so, delay matters . . . But it is all so *vague*." He continued, even more slowly,

"I think I had better speak with Thomas, too. If you will agree. Our only hope of further discovery seems through him, at least at present. That is, unless, of course, you feel you can do better with him yourself?"

"No, indeed. He seems to me to be at least half in sympathy with these plotters, and I imagine you, as a man he respects (rather than I, a mere woman in his mind—even a child still), could perhaps explain to him the—the *risks* that honest though misguided folk are running . . . that they are allying themselves with less scrupulous men, and less worthy causes. If we could thus enlist his aid even to a small degree, it would be a great help . . ."

There was no time for more. Lord Barton was already to be heard in the corridor outside, and next moment was again with them, Mr. Tregannan close behind; and Maria, too, who unwittingly, it would seem, allayed any suspicions Mr. Tregannan might have had about Thea and Miles's being alone together by saying, in satisfied tones,

"Well, I did not have to go far for my warm shawl after all. It was just outside here, on the old press. I must send Stukely to call the girls, they will be searching everywhere in my boudoir by now!"

The evening fell into its usual pattern and, quite early, the guests departed to their separate homes.

The next day, as Thea and Miles had contrived, Miles spoke in the privacy of the harness room to Thomas. Miles himself leaned casually at ease in an attempt to make the odd conversation seem as informal as possible. But Thomas was an old servant, and stood rigidly to attention, his sturdy independence not at all diminished, but his sense of fitness well to the fore, and his expression verging on the disapproving.

"Thomas, I am not your master, I have no claim on your time, and I will attempt to be as brief as possible. Firstly, I want to make it clear that I do not believe in any form of coercion . . . in any forced obedience," Miles explained hastily, seeing the blank look on the coachman's face, "and what I am about to say to you now, as well as how you answer me, will be forgotten by me instantly if you do not agree with what is said. Neither Miss Thea, who, as you know, wishes me to speak with you, nor I, will hold your sentiments against you, but will consider the matter closed: I cannot preface my remarks plainer than that. And I hope you know me for a man of honor."

Thomas, unused to being so addressed by the gentry, cleared his throat and said, gruffly, that he had always known Mr. Barrett to be a gentleman of his word; and that, anyway, he was Mr. Langham's friend, and Miss Thea spoke for him, "And that is quite enough for me, sir."

Thus adjured, as it were, Miles struggled to make the situation, as he and Thea saw it, clear.

"I think you were not here, some years ago, when the Lancashire Luddite weavers, and rioters generally, fired many mills, broke machinery, destroyed steam and power looms, and private houses even, and generally ran wild ... Some men were killed, some maimed, and a great deal of trouble and sorrow was caused to quite innocent people, of all classes. Elsewhere in the Midlands it was even worse . . . and continues still, sporadically!"

Thomas agreed not to have been present, but attending to his duties with his master, Mr. Langham, in Surrey. But he had heard tell of these and similar outbreaks, of far greater violence, in Nottinghamshire, Yorkshire, and Durham. He added, without aggression, "The risings or whatever you call them were put down hereabouts most cruelly, sir, folk said. And some were, after all, about food, not machinery! Indeed, same as what you said for t'other side—when the magistrates and the soldiery got going, the innocent could get hurt, one way or another, often as not, along with the guilty."

"I agree with you, Thomas, there was bad spirit on *both* sides—some say deliberately fanned, by men of ill will, on *both* sides. But what I want to point out now is that, although rioting and burning continues intermittently in some counties, it has been quiet here in Lancashire for two years. It's possible, I suppose, that local Luddites, being sensible fellows, have no stomach for such fights and punishments ever again here and hope to improve matters by more peaceful means. But, either way, normal citizens, and countrymen of all walks of life here, are in favor of such peace and quiet; and the happier for it. Of *that* I am convinced."

Thomas said nothing. And Miles, thinking perhaps to discern a faint antagonism, continued with more force,

"But whether *that* point is arguable or not, there is something which must be said: I, and several others, have reason to believe that more trouble is planned here, in this region, in the near future . . . Indeed, I myself have been indirectly threatened . . ."

At this, the coachman looked up, obviously disturbed and surprised, as Miles had expected him to be. He was quick, therefore, to seize his advantage and add, forcefully,

"What makes matters worse is that we learn that the influential, and quite probably the greater, number of these . . . plotters . . . are not Luddites at all . . . They are a mixture—you have my word on it—of vicious opportunists out for spoils, or of men who wish for a differently ordered society—perhaps to overthrow the monarchy and replace it with some sort of republic, like the

French. There may even (though I can't be certain), be other French trouble-makers fanning the flames too. Many responsible people believe that some in France will not keep the peace much longer and so would dearly like to have us in internal disarray when they renew their hostilities."

Here Miles considered adding that others among the agents provocateurs might well be British government spies, set up to inflame trouble and infiltrate the Luddite groups and then (being knowledgeable of their plans) catch the ringleaders in the act. But this seemed refining too much upon the matter for his audience and might well so confuse Thomas as to undo all the good his homily had so far done. He therefore desisted, waiting in silence for the man's reaction.

This was long in coming, but eventually the coachman raised his head and, looking levelly at Miles, said slowly,

"As I knows you to be a sound man, sir, and not given to light speech about such matters, I must needs believe you. And what it comes to, to my way of thinking, is that simple men with an honest grievance are going to be used and penalized by rogues employing that grievance as a cover for . . . for selfish or treacherous ends—and treacherous deeds, maybe."

"You have the matter exactly, Thomas!"

"So what are you asking of me to do, then?" The query came with typical directness. Followed at once by a cynical if half-hearted, "Betray my friends, who *do* have an honest grievance?"

"No. But perhaps if you could . . . listen carefully when you are with such company. And let me know of anything suspicious, or planned—probably within a sennight—

in this region. And, at the end, if you felt sure of them, perhaps you could warn your friends to keep away and tell them why. For most of them are, undoubtedly loyal Englishmen. But to be honest, I should much prefer, for the moment, if you would merely keep your eyes and ears open, and your mouth shut . . . Unless, that is, you know of—well—anything of importance already?"

"I knows nothing, sir. Merely some of them whispering behind their hands, as it were. I takes no part, deliberate, you see."

"Well, will you try to, now? Time is so short, Thomas. We have but six days." He did not add, "And I myself but four."

Another long pause. Then Thomas said, deliberately devious, or so it seemed,

"Miss Thea thought to be returning home after tomorrow, sir, remember? And I drives her."

"Yes, yes. We had thought of that. But she is willing, nay, anxious, to delay her return for at least a week longer. If we are to the right of it, you see, *something* is to occur within a week. And we would hope to avert it for many reasons. Miss Thea will speak with you too, if you wish it. Or even allow you to return to Ewell, perhaps, if you have no stomach for the affair. I will help you all I can, of course, but it would seem to be you, at present anyway, who has the . . . the entré to the plotters, and who runs a consequent risk. . ." He thought it best to add, frankly,

"We could, of course, inform official military and civil authorities up here now, at once. But we have so little to go on, and I feel we may then, by doing so, by presenting them with such . . . nebulous . . . suspicions, either precipitate matters, perhaps bloodily, or drive the plotters underground for a space. Neither of these seems, to me, a satisfactory solution. If we can but find out *something* of the conspiracy first, we may be able to avert a tragedy. I too, have a source of information, you see, though hardly like to prove as fruitful as yours, and I would wish to look further into it."

There was another long pause. Until Thomas said, quietly,

"No need of further talk, sir. I rather think I agree with you. So I'll see at once what I can find out about anything. But you must give me, later, leave to do as I think about my . . . my real friends."

The curious meeting ended. Miles returned to find Thea and tell her that it had been, in the main, successful; and to advise her to send word at once to Surrey, upon some harmless pretext or other, that she planned to delay her departure from the north for a few days longer, so that Mr. Langham should not be worried. There was little more they could profitably discuss. They agreed upon four days to try, by any means that came to hand, to discover more of the mystery. But after that, they both felt, their knowledge must be put in the hands of local military and civil authorities, however little actual evidence they possessed, however clumsily matters might be handled by these authorities, and whatever the outcome might be—to Miles personally and to others.

Chapter 15

IT must be true that God or, as the New Thought would have it, Fate, at least sometimes directs our actions, if not our destiny. Thea was an excellent horsewoman, neat, precise, daring, yet never overly wild, who knew to a 'T' when to take a chance and when to avoid one. Jumps, both high and wide, held no terrors for her or Silver, and, not to labor matters further, she had almost forgotten when she had last had a fall, so long ago was it. However, the afternoon of the day following Miles's talk with Thomas, Fate overtook her. She was galloping easily along a ridge far from the Bartons', when Silver's hoof caught in some unknown obstruction—a rabbit hole, perhaps, or one of those grass-hidden bits of rock so frequent on the hillsides —and the mare fell heavily, only just avoiding rolling on Thea herself. Shaking, her shoulder aching as though dislocated, Thea rose, turning her attention, for all her pain, to her beloved Silver. She was standing again, but with head down and bridle trailing, close by. A cautious examination revealed the mare was badly lamed: it was obvious she could not even be walked any distance, let alone ridden, but would need a conveyance to take her back to the stables, and salves for her injury.

Thea looked about her anxiously. Below, seen from the ridge, lay the town, and the livery stables where Miles Barrett, William Barton, and therefore, she herself were well known. Snaking down to the town was a narrow, muddily rutted, and extremely winding path. The Bartons' house was, on the other hand, a good seven miles distant, any shorter return being separated by cloughs, rocky outcrops, and streams; and Miles Barrett's was still farther, even as the crow flies. Thea knew enough of the terrain to be certain an attempted short cut, among the scattered boulders, walls, woods, and deep hidden valleys, was certain suicide. Miles's house she did not even consider. So, tying Silver to a tree stump to prevent her attempting to follow her mistress, talking to her soothingly, and throwing the cape of her fashionable riding habit over her for warmth, (though fortunately today the weather was both mild and dry), she set off on the track towards the town.

Inwardly, Thea berated herself roundly for refusing a groom. Everyone, at some time or another, had remonstrated with her about this, predicting various disasters from attack to accident, but she had never heeded them. Now, indeed, they had been proved right. She walked on, realizing with increasing dismay that the distance was a good deal farther than she had thought, the turns and twists (seen from above as mere nothings) were far longer and more winding when traversed on foot, and she became aware, too, that it would be dusk before she reached her destination. Her shoulder was now aching abominably, and although she had no real fear for her mare, knowing her to be obedient to command, and well sheltered by a thick tree, with grass to crop, she yet felt unhappy at the long delay before she could be aided. Constantly, her eyes sought some form of habitation where she might perhaps hire a mount of some sort, or a nag and cart, or even a youth to run to her destination and get aid more quickly. There was nothing and no one.

The light began to fail early; probably more rain was on the way, she thought angrily. It was, she supposed, just possible she would be missed from the Bartons', but William was so occupied with his affairs, and Maria so casual. Anyway, she had herself to blame that no one ever expected to see her indoors on a reasonable day, or would think to look for her until quite late. She realized, bitterly, that being a law unto herself (although with her indulgent friend Maria's complete agreement) had its disadvantages. Where could they begin to search? She might have taken any of several bridle tracks, and she was known, moreover to stray often from these, as the mood took her. Poor Silver! She paused to support her aching shoulder with a kind of sling adapted from the scarf of her riding hat, then hurried on as fast as possible.

Nevertheless, it was indeed dusk when she eventually arrived on the edge of the town. Worse, she found herself in an area of squalid streets that she had not known existed (although the place was small) and therefore could not immediately find her direction toward the stables she sought. Seeing no one to ask, however, she took what she thought to be the correct way, walking more slowly now in spite of herself, for she was weary, the narrow street was abominably cobbled, and her shoulder pained her badly. She had the uncomfortable feeling of being watched from the mean houses and hovels on each side but told herself firmly that this foolish sensation was probably only due to her imagination. Besides, she must by now look indeed a sight, with her hat long since gone, her boots and habit muddy, her hair awry, and her arm in a sling. She resolved all the same not to knock upon any doors, but to wait until she could ask the first person she met with if, indeed, she were set right for Poulton's Livery Stables.

She was not exactly certain at what moment she began to suspect she was being followed. It was difficult in the dusk to make out anything tangible. But from time to time she became aware of a light footfall and, looking back, thought to glimpse a movement, a wisp of skirt perhaps, disappearing into one of the many dark, narrow alleyways that ran into the street on both sides. The feeling was uncanny—sinister—and heightened, she realized, by the emptiness of the street she was walking along. It was strange, she thought: in London, an area such as this would be, if not teeming, at least reasonably peopled. Perhaps it was just that such folk as these among the Northerners were, as people said, dour, and kept to themselves. All the same it seemed a brooding quiet. Turning another corner, for no firm reason she deliberately waited a moment, then swung back suddenly . . . and came face to face with a woman, sallow, thin-faced, with piercing dark eyes, and a forehead prematurely lined, for she could not have been much more than Thea's own age.

She also realized there was nothing to be apprehensive of, at least, not in the thin, almost wasted figure before her. Truth to tell, the other woman appeared the more fearful of the two, for she kept glancing behind her and from side to side. Then she dragged Thea, who succumbed from sheer surprise, back around the corner into the street she had just entered, and thence into yet another little arched alleyway. She said in a thick mutter, her broad vowels making her difficult to understand, even by Thea, who by now was accustomed to the local way of speaking through the Bartons' servants.

"Th'art Mistress Langham, aren't thee?" Then, not waiting for an answer, she went on, "Ah seed thee, coming through the Bartons' servants,

"And what if I was?" demanded Thea coldly, getting a word in at last, and beginning, perhaps through pain and weariness, to resent this peculiar approach. But if the woman detected any such resentment, she ignored it, being more fearful, Thea suddenly realized, for herself than for Thea. She peered back out of the alley, muttering again.

"Eh, they munt see me wi' thee, leastways not me 'usband and 'is like!" Then she began to shiver, so that Thea, caught between an inexplicable sense of fear for herself and sympathy for the stranger, asked urgently,

"What is it then? Have you something to tell me?"

"Aye!" The compelling dark eyes in the aging young face stared directly into hers. "That I 'ave! My man—he's a friend of your coachman—they've nowt in common, really, save ale, but they *like* one another." Here the woman stopped, and gazed again, in a kind of mesmerized terror, at Thea, who said, instinctively caught in an atmosphere of urgency as well as fear,

"Well, go *on*."

"My man's a fool, mistress. Not *bad*—just . . . well . . . cheerful and easy led! Th'as likely knowed some thyself . . ."

"Have I not!" agreed Thea grimly. The two regarded each other in a new, equal, women's alliance.

"Not that he hasn't real cause to hate." The woman stopped abruptly, then said, again shortly. "They don't want our work any more at t'mill, see? 'Aven't for long since. We used to work at home, see, and take what we did up to t'mill. But with these new-fangled machines they don't need us any more. He's *tried* for work . . . but he's nowt to do but loaf . . . ripe for mischief!"

Thea, who already suspected what this encounter referred to, desperate for information, and now likely to drop with pain and fatigue, yet managed to keep her voice calm and civil.

"I beg you, tell me *quickly,* what you have to say! My horse is up there injured, and I myself. . ." she pointed to her makeshift sling.

A crease of sympathy marred the already lined forehead, and the woman tut-tutted. But her life having obviously been one of dealing with major disasters first, and ignoring lesser ills, she took no more notice of Thea's own plight, continuing her own story urgently.

"Sam, that's my husband, 'as got another friend. Evil, dangerous, wi' a tongue like silk. A paddy called Mick, from Liverpool . . . Sam'll do most anything 'e asks 'im to . . . Well, summat's afoot . . . And your coachman, he was down at the tavern late this very day, at a quiet time like, plying my man wi' drink and . . . and asking 'im *questions*. It's my belief he's onto us."

"How do you know all this?"

"Barmaid's my sis. She saw 'em, in a corner. Swears no one else of . . . well, of any importance, far as we're concerned, was there. But sent to warn me."

"And why do you feel I can . . . I mean, why speak to *me?*"

" 'E's *your* servant. *Someone* put 'im up to asking Sam questions privatelike, 'e never 'as before. You was seen, yesterday, in town, watching 'em all."

("Who," thought Thea, "who saw me? The crossing sweeper? The little maid who was attending to the fire and the lamp in the dark milliner's shop? The milliner, herself? Who 'saw' me, and told of it?" She suddenly felt cold.)

"You don't 'ave to worry," the woman said, sardonically, perhaps noticing Thea's shiver, "since they don't know your servant's been pumping away at my man . . . you were just a—sort of chance mention. And I'll see they don't know. Sis'll hold *her* tongue, she don't like some of her customers, see, and my poor fool don't even realize he *was* being pumped!" She looked up, her face set suddenly in hard lines.

"But *I* want to know what you're at! I'm that throng, I can't make up my mind! Sometimes I feel you've a kind of concern for us. Others, I reckon if you'd known or discovered owt, you, or your sort'd be round to the military or the magistrates like a shot. Is that what your servant, my Sam's *'friend'* is doing? Finding out? So you can split to the ———— magistrates?"

It was the first foul word she had used; and heaven knows, thought Thea, she must have heard enough since her earliest days. It showed the extent of her involvement, at least for her husband's sake, and her potential for dangerous dealings. Leaning back wearily against the damp, moss-grown, evil-smelling wall to ease her fatigue, she looked gravely into the woman's eyes.

"Tell me, Mrs.——"

"Schofield, if you must know."

"Tell me, Mrs. Schofield, do you agree with . . . violence? Burning and breaking, rioting . . . even killing? And the results, the retribution they ultimately bring to those who behave so?"

"I saw enough of it in these parts in 1812, thank you. And heard of worse elsewhere. No. I don't. But," she added harshly, "I don't blame them as does it. Not really. I don't believe in starvation either, see, or work being taken away from honest folk like us!"

It was an honest answer.

"Nor do I," said Thea. She closed her eyes as a wave of pain and despair swept over her, and she wondered hopelessly how she had best deal with the astute woman before her. Feeling her way, she began slowly.

"You have been honest with me. Will you take it, on my oath, that I am being equally honest with you? If it will help your husband?" she added, cautiously.

Mrs. Schofield eyed her with equal caution. She said, guardedly,

"Say what you have to, and we'll see. And best be brief. It'll not go well with me if I'm found hobnobbing with you. And you're like to collapse any minute. But you'll get no help from me if you do—much as my life's worth. So?"

Thea said slowly, "We quite literally stumbled on a mysterious plot from another source. But we knew—

know—nothing more about it. You must believe me, it was quite by chance I saw the group outside the tavern yesterday. There was, however, one man I recognized— from the other source, as it were: the man with the brogue you say is from Liverpool."

"And who is 'we,' miss, if I may make so bold?"

"A . . . a landowner, a good man and discreet. A friend of mine . . ." She stopped, and this time it was Mrs. Schofield's turn to ask, but angrily and impatiently,

"Well, go on."

"Your Irishman is associated in this plot, whatever it may be, with a far more dangerous man, seemingly a gentleman. And this friend of mine is being . . ." Realizing she was becoming incoherent, possibly indiscreet, she took a deep breath, and began again.

"And this extremely dangerous man is attempting to force a friend of mine, through cruel blackmail, to aid them in some secret fashion . . . Only I fear a great deal more is involved than honest men rioting for what should rightly be theirs, ma'am. Revolutionaries, republicans, foreigners, many others will *use* your honest Luddites here—" she brought out the word boldly—"to their own ends. And you can imagine how heavily, ultimately, the government will, rightly, punish *any* who disturb the peace. They will regard it as treason."

"And who are *ye* concerned for, miss? Your friend or us Luddites?"

"Both," said Thea simply.

"So what is your coachman doing *spying?*"

"We, this friend and I, thought that if we could find out more about the plot, we might threaten the black-mailer (who is undoubtedly their leader) with our knowledge, and so insure the collapse of the plot. A collapse without violence—which means without resort to civil, or worse, military authority. We have but four days, Mrs. Schofield. I cannot explain why. Then, as good patriots, although personally I . . . we . . . feel *your* grievance is a just one, we shall have to inform the authorities of the little we actually know. I cannot answer for how *they* will behave."

Thea swayed. Mrs. Schofield who, it occurred to Thea in a dazed way, had turned from frightened nonentity into a positive dragon, merely put out her hand and steadied her by pressing her against the wall. She stared at Thea with those bright, sunken eyes, as if to see into her very soul. At last she said, slowly,

"I think you're honest. I believe what you say, so far as it goes. And I wanted no truck with this silly violence *afore* what you told me about foreigners and the like. No one *uses* us!" She drew herself up, but then added, with unconscious pathos,

"But I *know* nothing! Sam is a fool with his friends, but he won't tell *me*. Maybe he's been warned! All he's said to me is that he has an important part to play, poor idiot! He has to signal with a lighted torch when he's told to. Maybe," she added gloomily, "that's all *he* knows!"

"Perhaps, if he does know more—a date or place even —he will say so to Thomas!"

The woman's head came up sharply. "And if he *does* . . . what's to become of him—of us?"

Thea replied, with a force born of desperation. "I swear that, if you can keep him from any . . . affray, or even if he is involved, I personally, through this friend of mine, will intervene and plead for an amnesty for him!"

Mrs. Schofield gazed again at her. The powerful country gentry, as she still recognized it, stared back at her. She said, briefly, dismissively,

"All right. I trust you. If I do hear aught—and I'll try —I'll get word to you. As you to me. Through that coachman of yourn. And whatever happens, I'll hold you to your word, miss, about my Sam. Now, you'd best go." She gave Thea a push. "Straight on up the road for nigh on ten minutes, and you gain the High Street. Right by the stables. My best road lies the other way."

She pointed down the alley they were hidden in. Hardly aware of what she was doing, Thea staggered on.

Chapter 16

W HILE *Thea had been struggling through her ordeal,* Miles, too, had been occupied. It was purely fortuitous that Sir Humphrey, his elder brother, called on him early that same afternoon about a business matter, some small legal complication within the family, that needed Miles's signature. He had ridden over, therefore, leaving his wife Hannah behind, and proposed, if Miles were agreeable, to spend the night at his brother's and return the following day.

Although the brothers had never been very close, there was an easy relationship between them: neither censured nor resented the other. Indeed, any stiffness between them was invariably caused solely by Hannah who, when she was present, seemed almost miraculously capable of putting her finger on some unknown or long forgotten sore spot, so that the ease of their companionship was at once broken. Privately, Miles opined that she did this deliberately, her jealousy resenting even a rapport between brothers. But for Humphrey's sake he invariably ruled his sarcastic tongue and minded his temper in her presence. However, it was far pleasanter to receive his brother without his wife, and the two men, needing a witness to Miles's signature on the document, agreed to ride over to the Rector, whom they felt would be preferable to one of the upper servants in this case.

Fortunately, for Humphrey was inwardly of the opinion that he had ridden far enough that day, the distance was short: but ten minutes through the home park and then, briefly along the village street to the Reverend Begby, a pleasant if rather worldly bachelor with an excellent taste in port. They were about to turn into the short gravel drive before the white, bow-fronted rectory, when another rider passed along the street rather fast, with a brief bow in their direction. Miles's brows drew together. He had *seen* enough of Jeremy Tregannan already; what he needed now, was to *know* more about him. Humphrey, however, said in puzzled tones as they rode up to the semicircular entry steps of the rectory,

"Who is that? His face seems somehow familiar!"

Miles looked at his brother sharply. "If you have the least idea, Humphrey, I wish you would concentrate and tell me! He is the bane—nay, worse—of my existence at present. I speak in confidence and will explain this evening."

Humphrey, however, had only time to turn in surprise and regard the dark look on his brother's face when the door was opened by Mr. Begby's housekeeper, the two visitors ushered within, and their horses led away by the stable boy. The Reverend Mr. Begby was a formal fellow, with all the time in the world to indulge this whim: to Miles, never had the formalities seemed so long, nor the conversation so slow, nor even the port so unpalatable. But Humphrey, aware of his brother's anxiety and impatience, pleaded weariness, and at last they were able to leave with the document properly witnessed. Once outside, Humphrey said, however, in a worried voice,

"I can't place that man. Who does he *say* he is?"

"He claims to be a Jeremy Tregannan, gentleman, and has leased Yew Tree Mansion at the opposite end of the village from Begby. I suspect, however, that he is a Frenchman, possibly a Jacobin. The more so because he was in Paris last year, and maybe earlier . . . Also, of course, he *looks* like a Frenchman, just as some Englishmen are unmistakably English, and some Prussians, Prussian!" This was said half jokingly, yet with a bitter edge to his voice quite unlike Miles. Once again Humphrey glanced at his younger brother in surprise. After this, they rode the rest of the way in silence, Humphrey obviously in deep concentration, which Miles did not attempt to break. At last, when they were comfortably seated before a great fire, Humphrey looked up with a satisfied smile,

"I have it! That's no Frenchman, Miles, he's as English as you are! He is, or was, a fatherless young man, a commoner, who used to live with his mother in some factory cottages put up about ten miles from my estates by an eccentric, widowed mill owner. Why, I often used to speak of the old man! Half-dotty, true, but benevolent, with deep radical ideas. A nice enough fellow, as manufacturers go, and rolling in what he used to call 'brass.' But impossible socially, of course. Unless you'd not a feather to fly with, or an elderly spinster daughter to dispose of!"

"Never mind the useless wit and light-minded speculation, Humphrey! What about Tregannan?"

Humphrey, realizing something even more was at stake than he had thought, took no offense at his brother's tone. He went on slowly,

"The youngster's name wasn't Tregannan then, of course. Can't you remember *what* it was . . . but he was about eighteen at the time, bright, a 'likely lad' as they say in our parts, with a pleasing manner. Thewliss, the mill owner, who had no children, took him under his wing. Had him tutored—seems he was an apt pupil and had a quick ear. Anyway, he made, as far as possible, a gentleman out of him, and then put him to work in a responsible position in the mill . . . Some said then he was destined to be the elderly man's heir, in default of a real one . . . I don't know."

"But then something happened?"

"Not at once. Everything rolled along as smoothly as a machine. Indeed, more smoothly than one, you might say these days! The mother died. The protégé moved into the Big House. He seemed to love . . . indeed, let us speak fairly, *did* love his benefactor. The only thing was that he became known, locally, for his radicalism. Though that was not surprising, I suppose, when you think of Thewliss's own ideas. Anyway, the young man went about speaking against mill owners and manufacturers of all kinds except —and he made this clearly known—his own benefactor whom, he said, he revered as a good man and a good master. But there were no other good ones, or so it seemed to your Tregannan."

"And Thewliss permitted this?"

"He humored the boy, poor old fool! He loved him and perhaps—who knows?—he thought the wildness would pass, as it does, one way or another, with all young men! Or maybe his pride was tickled, as well as his own professed radicalism, to be considered so enlightened and different from the rest of his kind." Humphrey paused, staring into the heart of the fire, then went on,

"Anyway, considerably later, the rioting began, and the machine-breaking, the firing of buildings—you know what Yorkshire was like, even near the start of the Luddite movement! Frankly, I don't know whether this Tregannan, as you call him, had a hand in it—apart from the previous long period of his inflammatory speeches—or not. Quite possibly not, at first. But then, Thewliss was killed in one of the early riots, by a group of fire-raisers from a different part of the county. They fired his house and he, being elderly, was asphyxiated."

Miles looked up quickly. But Humphrey raised his hand.

"No. Not what you're thinking. Your Tregannan had no part in it, he was actually away in London, getting orders, at the time. This was proven. He appears to have been exceedingly distressed by the affair. Indeed, it seems the tragedy also served to unhinge him somewhat. I'd say he became addled in his wits . . . for he blamed the bad mill owners (and remember, this meant *all* other owners) for the tragedy—insisted if they had all been like Thewliss, with cottages built, and compensation, of some sort or another, for work lost, no risings would have taken place. . ." Humphrey shrugged his shoulders. "He did inherit, incidentally, and sold up but did not immediately move away, becoming deliberately active in the rioting, both financing the Luddite cause, and organizing its activities in various areas."

"If all this was known, why then was he not apprehended?"

"It's known *now*, old fellow. It wasn't then, only suspected. His fellow conspirators were loyal. Anyway, he could never be found to apprehend. Actually, he brought attention on himself, dramatically, by murdering a particularly vicious mill owner in cold blood, and with cold steel. Well," Humphrey conceded, "that's not exactly correct. Again it was *suspected* who had done the deed but not proved. Nobody come forward; nobody would inform; and frankly, everyone, perhaps even the law, in this case, didn't really care, the general feeling being that this particular mill owner had got his just deserts."

"And so?"

"Well, the whole area had obviously, all the same, become too hot for Tregannan. He vanished, was never seen again, and that was the end of the matter."

As he said this, Humphrey looked sidewise at his brother, an old, odd, three-cornered look that Miles remembered from long ago as a child. He said impatiently,

"Come on, there's more!"

"Not really," replied Humphrey calmly. "I am a magistrate myself, as you know, and was then, so this next information came to me privately: Tregannan, or someone very like him, suddenly turned up attempting to incite to riot in the agricultural Southeast of England. And here, there *was* a suspected tie-in with the French, although the authorities could not be certain and never have been. Still, Tregannan was then considered potentially so dangerous, we being still at war with the French, that a renewed attempt to apprehend him on the earlier murder charge, at least, was made. I believe they even called the Runners in. In fact, I am sure of it. But he was slippery, it seems, as well as dangerous. Nothing developed. He was never found."

Humphrey stopped. "That's all I know. And I'll have you bear in mind, Miles, that all this took place years ago. Callow youths change in their twenties, and I might well have mistaken the man I saw today for him. I saw him close only once, you know, during one of his rabble-rousing periods when he ran afoul of me. Now tell me, why is he so much in your mind?"

About to embark, with some difficulty, on the recent story of Jeremy's intrigues, both known and suspected—including Georgina's disgrace—Miles stopped short. Fond as he was of Humphrey, he yet recalled that his brother's indisputable discretion did not extend to Hannah: he always had—and always would—talk to his wife. And although, perhaps, she would attach little importance to any talk of plots, and would maintain the silence her husband would undoubtedly ask for on such matters, Miles could well imagine how she would enjoy a discreet destruction, under the guise of sworn secrecy and pity, of Georgina's reputation among her friends. He said instead, therefore, with some apology in his voice,

"I'm sorry, Humphrey. I think perhaps it's best to say nothing at present, after all. You have not fully identified the man, and it would be unfair, as well as incautious, to speak further until we have more information."

Humphrey regarded his younger brother for an instant, his fierce blue eyes under their rather shaggy brows, bleak and intimidating. Then, suddenly, he laughed.

"All right! I can't guess why this sudden caution—unless it's unfit for Hannah's ears," he added, with an unfathomable grin. "But I'll not take offense—though I've a mind to!"

Miles smiled back gratefully. Then, on a sudden inspiration, he asked,

"Do you think, in view of the Runners' involvement, Bow Street knows any more than you have told me?"

"It's possible. Although you'll never get them to disgorge, I'll tell you that. At least not without showing your hand, which you've obviously no mind to!"

Miles agreed, absently, that it was probably true that in such a case the Runners would give no information. But he was thinking otherwise. Like many a younger son, he had spent a couple of years in the Brigade; had, indeed, seen service, briefly, in the Peninsula. And a friend of his from that time, another ex-Guardee, was, he knew, a close friend of James Read, the officer in charge of the Runners. . . . If only he had a little more time, he could set off quickly for London and attempt, through the good offices of his old army friend, to gain more useful information about Tregannan. For that Jeremy and this will-o'-the-wisp of Humphrey's were one and the same, he was well-nigh certain.

The brothers spent a casual, comfortable evening together, Humphrey fortunately, from Miles's point of view, retiring early. For during that evening Miles had privately come to a decision, and had hasty preparations to make: he intended going to London, despite the meager time at his disposal.

Chapter 17

*T*HE *morning after her ordeal, Thea had somewhat re-*
covered. The Livery Stables, appalled to see a favored
member of the gentry in such a state, had at once bustled
about. A doctor had been called in, Lord Barton notified
by messenger, and when he arrived on horseback, his
mount flecked with foam and sweat, a coach was put at his
disposal to convey Thea to his house; and Silver had been
recovered from the ridge.

Next morning, therefore, the wrench in her shoulder
having proved less severe than at first thought, Thea had,
in spite of Maria's remonstrances, insisted on dressing and
descending to the drawing room, where she ordered
Thomas to attend her and also asked for a messenger to be
sent early to Miles informing him of her accident, for she
wanted, naturally, to tell him as quickly as possible about

her encounter with Mrs. Schofield. The first demand, for
Thomas, was looked on somewhat askance by William.
Surely Thea would not wish to go driving today? But Thea
was ready for this and said, looking as much as she could
like an inexperienced young woman, that she *must* see
Thomas, both to get precise news of Silver's condition,
and to explain personally to her coachman—for he had
instructed her in horsemanship years ago, and she was
very fond of him and valued his opinion—how the accident
had occurred. Her hints to Maria that Miles should know
as soon as possible of her accident were understood and
agreed to at once, her sentimental friend seeing the hoped-
for romance approaching fruition and willing to do everything in her power to further this end.

Thus it turned out that Miles, his departure for London
delayed by news of Thea, arrived while Thomas was still
with his mistress. Entering the room, Miles heartily wished
the coachman elsewhere, for the sight of Thea, fragile, her
eyes huge in her wan face, with her arm bound by a scarf
against her breast, inspired in him an almost violent wish
to comfort and caress her. Thomas would at once have
withdrawn, but Thea, flashing a quick, warm smile at
Miles, said hastily,

"No, Thomas! Tell your story to Mr. Barrett before you
leave, if you please!"

Thus instructed, Thomas had nothing for it (though
vastly uncomfortable at the look which crossed Miles's
face) but to turn to the newcomer and embark again on his
discoveries made the previous day. It seemed he had lurked
in town, hoping to see Sam Schofield loafing about as usual,
and have a private exploratory talk with him,

"Pump him tactful—like, sir," was how Thomas put it. "For he's a friend of mine, and a nice enough cove, if a bit weak-willed. Not simple, exactly, but he's got a loose tongue, and if handled tactful, runs on to anyone he likes and trusts, without even knowing he's giving matters away that had best, for those concerned, often not be spoken of."

Miles nodded, and the coachman continued with his tale. Finding his crony without himself being observed had proved unexpectedly easy, it seemed. He was walking cautiously down the narrow lane that led to one of Schofield's haunts, the tavern, when he saw his quarry ahead of him, slipping into the back of the alehouse. Going himself to the window and peering cautiously in, Thomas saw, as he had expected, Sam Schofield with his sister-in-law, obviously "on the scrounge" for free ale when no one was about the place.

"Well, sir, I knows Alice, Sam's wife's sister, and she's tight-mouthed, as buttoned-up as they make 'em . . . well, best kind of beer wenches got to be, sir (though I don't expect you'll be knowing about that) 'cos what some men will say under the influence, to a kind female face a'front them . . ." He stopped, glanced at Thea a little abashed, and then went on, "What's more to the point, she's no time for these plotters and trouble-makers, that I *can* tell you certain-sure, no need to go into detail . . . so, making sure the innkeeper ain't around, who I *don't* count among my friends, I just nips in too, and asks Alice, respectful and private-like, if I can have a word with Sam. And if she'd forget she'd seen me afterwards." He grinned, "She give me a rather queer look, but agrees. So there I am, unseen, alone with him!"

Again Thomas glanced shrewdly at his audience. "It's

my belief he don't know much, because if *I* knows he runs at the mouth, so too must his fellow conspirators. All the same, I did glean some information."

This, with many necessary explanations and unnecessary circumlocutions, came to the fact that an uprising of some sort was indeed already organized, but delayed, since a cache of what Thomas took to be firearms could not be obtained until paid for. The size or whereabouts of this cache he had no idea of, but suspected it to be a pretty substantial one from Sam's grouse that, God knew, there were enough of the things, and yet he was only to be trusted with a torch, not a shooter. "When he said that, sir, that's when I realized arms were involved."

Miles nodded. "And the torch he *is* to be trusted with: he is to fire something perhaps?"

"I think not," interposed Thea, unexpectedly. "From what his wife said to me, he is to *signal* with it. But I cannot be sure, of course. He could even be setting fire to something as a signal—ricks, buildings?"

Miles, a little dazed at all the activity reported by Thea and her coachman, nevertheless decided to get Thomas's story finished first.

"You could not contrive to gain any information about time or place, Thomas?"

"Place, no, sir. Only indirectly, for when Sam was complaining about the firearms, he said that two men had visited his more fortunate cronies with a sample shooter to show them how to use the things. And they talked so queer and thick, they probably wouldn't be able to understand, or give, orders if asked to."

"Foreigners?"

"Not what you and me call foreigners, no, sir," said

Thomas, as one man of the world to another. " 'E'd have said so. No, just not locals. From another county, perhaps."

Thea and Miles looked at each other. The Yorkshire visitors to the secret cottage? And from what part of Yorkshire did they come? From Huddersfield, say, where many ambitious coups were planned, and men trained perhaps, at least roughly, to handle weapons? The situation looked, indeed, serious. Without much hope in his voice, Miles asked again,

"I suspect it's asking too much of you, Thomas, to expect you to have gleaned anything on timing? Dates?"

Thomas looked smug. "Well, I've *something*, sir: it seems the leader, by the sound of it, for these parts anyway (couldn't get a name from Sam or even a hint of it, sir), was in a roaring rage the other night, on account of them firearms. Not usual with him, seemingly. Sam heard him from the kitchen of the tavern (where he shouldn't have been) when all was closed up and good folk asleep. Buyer and seller they were, having a real ding-dong. Seems the plotters missed the boat, like, not having the cash to hand. And the gun merchant (whoever he is) who's holding out for 'blunt first, guns after,' said he had to go away, so they got to wait longer now, till the end of the month before getting their hands on the shooters. Unexpected–like."

Miles put out his hand. "You've done excellently, Thomas. I congratulate you. But watch out for yourself. I only hope your friend Sam won't tumble to what you've been doing, and either deliberately or unintentionally, give away the fact that you *have* been, as you put it, 'pumping him.' "

"Oh, that's not likely, sir," said Thomas, with a vast

grin. "All I had to do was keep saying the words 'torch,' or 'shooter,' and all this fell into my hat, so to speak, along with his grievance, quite unsuspecting. Sam'll have forgotten he spoke of it by now, believe me!"

Miles, reflecting that there was nothing to equal the sharp intelligence and devious mind of the Cockney, congratulated him again, and then, as the coachman left, turned to Thea, relief in his eyes. "The end of the month! That has indeed given us more time, if Thomas is not mistaken in what he says, and I see no reason why he should be. It will give me the opportunity to investigate our friend Mr. Tregannan further." He then told Thea of Humphrey's chance information and of his own plans, including approaching the Runners through his old ex-Guardee friend.

"I intend to see Jeremy Tregannan immediately, pretending I have now definitely decided to aid him, for Georgina's sake. Indeed, that I am forced to do so. But that I shall have to go to London to raise the money he wants!"

He saw Thea's look of alarm and added comfortingly,

"Don't worry, I'll spin some convincing yarn. I can't lag behind your simple Thomas in subtlety and duplicity for a good cause, can I?"

This made Thea laugh, but so fragile did she look, so overset and harassed, that Miles knelt suddenly beside her and, taking both her hands in his, said in his deep, now gentle voice, "My poor child, you should be in bed!"

But Thea, anxious to tell him of her meeting with Sam Schofield's wife, glanced again at him with that feverish glitter instead of her usually cool gaze and said hastily, ignoring his gentleness,

"Quickly, before anyone comes! I have something to tell

you, too!" She then began her story, only half aware, so immersed was she in it, that Miles had moved to the sofa beside her, his slender yet strong brown hands holding hers. When she was finished, however, it was another matter: she glanced at his face, then down at his hands; the hectic flush faded, to leave her delicate countenance white, still, turned aside. He said, with that same gentleness, turning her face towards him,

"My dearest, dearest Thea. This is hardly the time to speak of it but . . . I have loved you so long—at first without realizing it, but for many months now, quite hopelessly."

As he spoke, her eyes had remained downcast, but now she looked up at him in surprise. He said, ruefully,

"You have shewn no . . . preference . . . for me. No extra warmth from your warm nature . . . but have loved me as impartially as all your other friends. Perhaps even less than Major Hodson!"

Thea remained staring into the dark, saturnine countenance that regarded her with such intensity. She said, slowly, "Major Hodson," and then began—with the memory of that staid, colorless, though worthy soldier in her mind—to laugh, wholeheartedly, naturally, her old self for the first time since Miles had seen her that day.

A sudden smile lightened his drawn, anxious face. He put his hand up to stroke her shining hair and suddenly bent, touching her lips briefly with his own. Her reaction was instantaneous and, as she clung to him with her uninjured arm, he kissed her again, fiercely, hungrily, all the loneliness since his wife's death and now his deep love for Thea herself fusing into one overwhelming emotion.

But there was little time for their absorption in each

other. Each drew apart, thinking of the sinister threat, still unknown, hanging over themselves and others. Miles said briefly, yet with some of his old jauntiness,

"I must leave without further delay. There is Tregannan to see and dupe, then, to London to see Captain Whittaker, late of His Majesty's Guards; then, hopefully, his friend James Read, chief of the Bow Street Runners."

But then he added, in a far different tone,

"When you are more recovered, will you look to Georgina for me while I am gone? I am disturbed for her."

Thea, who had herself been constantly worried at how little she knew of Miles's encounter with his daughter, and how Georgina went on, beyond the bare fact of her pregnancy, asked urgently,

"How is she, Miles? And how did you fare with her? I have not even been able to ask you—"

"Indeed, as it is barely two days since all this coil took place, and as we have been all that time so occupied on our separate urgent affairs, and never private, that is not surprising!"

He sighed, and said slowly, "It is no falsehood that she is confined to her bed. But rather due to her condition than to a chill—she is constantly sick at present. My housekeeper, Mrs. Horrocks, tells me this is quite usual. She is attending to her—a good, comfortable woman, the soul of discretion, too, whom I have known for years. Indeed, she came with Jane, my wife, and has remained ever since."

"You have told her the truth about Georgina's condition?"

Miles shrugged, "Of course. I could hardly keep it from her. But I trust her discretion and her resourcefulness, to keep the true facts, for now at least, from the staff. We have agreed that Georgina is supposed to have a fever and a putrid sore throat—so we are safe, too, from friendly visits at the moment. As for Georgina herself," he looked at Thea with infinite sadness, "she is quite unrepentant, still besotted with Tregannan, and will hear no word against him."

"Does she know of his deceit of her and his perfidious double-dealing?"

"I have not yet spoken to her of it . . . I *cannot,* Thea. And I think, from the little she has said to me—all in praise of him, of her certainty that he was, like herself carried away that one time, and intends, as soon as she is recovered from her 'chill,' to speak to me and ask for her hand—that she has no conception of it." He rose and turned to the mantel, gripping it tightly.

"I . . . I cannot disillusion her, Thea, if she is innocent in this. At least not yet . . . And if she knows more, and *is* deceiving us—for," he added bitterly, "after all, she herself has managed well enough in duplicity, has she not?—well, there is nought I can do at present, save tell her nothing of our suspicions or actions. That way, she is no threat to us or to herself. . . Let us give her the benefit of any doubt and allow her to keep her illusions a little longer, poor child."

Thea agreed sadly, a sudden memory of Georgina, so fresh, so young, begging her to pretend to be her friend, on their first meeting, "All the same, you cannot keep her incommunicado—from Jeremy, I mean—forever!"

Miles's face darkened. "No. But for, hopefully, a few more days. I should succeed in doing so! With Mrs.

Horrocks's help . . . and yours, my dear Thea, when you can!"

Thea considered. "I think it would be best, since you must go so suddenly, if I drive over this afternoon, ostensibly to see how Georgina's 'chill' is progressing, and once there, I can propose staying to keep her company until you return. It would be quite a normal thing to do. And that way Mrs. Horrocks will not be alone in her responsibility—we can share it. You must, of course," she added hastily, "explain to her beforehand about my arrival. Otherwise, if she is all you say she is, she will surely have me back in the carriage at once, and returned, smartly, to Maria and William!"

They laughed, but without much heart, for Georgina's sad future overshadowed them. However, Miles agreed with Thea that a friendly visit on her part was normal and would occasion no comment or query. His only concern was for Thea herself. "You are hardly well enough to rattle about in a carriage, my dearest!"

"Nonsense! I am known as a restless creature here. Perhaps all that placid contentment so apparent in Maria and William unsettles me!" Miles caught her hands again, and she smiled up suddenly, vividly, into his eyes as she continued, "I shall ask for their coach—you know, it is most excellently sprung, and the squabs are inches thick, so that this wretched shoulder won't be jolted—to go for a breath of air and to see Georgina. Maria won't refuse me. And then, once there, I shall elect to stay with her. Simple, you see!"

So it was arranged. Miles left, after a gentle farewell that caught at Thea's heart, first to return home and warn

Mrs. Horrocks that Thea was privy to the situation and soon to come to her aid; then to see Jeremy; and finally to ride as fast as possible to London.

Maria, entering the salon fussily, unable to contain her impatience any longer to see how the hoped-for romance was progressing, was sadly taken aback to find Miles already gone, and Thea composed, quite unlike any young woman who had just received a visit from a lover. It did not occur to her that Thea's calm was rather too monumental to be real.

Chapter 18

*A*T *the large fashionable posting inn on the Great North* Road, Miles ate a hasty meal while fresh mounts were saddled for him and his unwanted, unexpected cotraveler, now visible through the partition opposite, a thickset, cold-eyed man eating and drinking heartily in the tap room. The stranger could certainly ride, Miles reflected, and had so far been no hindrance whatsoever. At least Jeremy was correct in this. Indeed, as he went back in his mind over the last few hours, Miles had to admit to a certain grim amusement: he had called on Jeremy and succeeded, he was certain, in convincing him of his change of heart, chiefly, of course, because of Georgina. Jeremy had naturally scowled over the further delay in collecting the money, but had raised no objections. Miles's accounts of heavy debts incurred and unwilling bankers, necessitating his personal appearance at their place of business, was a masterpiece of deceit, though made credible, certainly, by his earlier reputation.

Jeremy had, however, retained both his caution and what he imagined to be the whip hand, by insisting that a 'friend' of his, a man he trusted absolutely, ride with Miles to London to make sure of no treachery or change of heart. This man could go, he insisted, as Miles's valet, and so stay in close and continual proximity to him without causing any comment whatsoever. In vain Miles insisted that he already had a valet; that his speed would be hampered by such a fellow traveler; and finally, that if he were saddled with such a man, he would not go at all. Jeremy had replied, imperturbably, that Miles could discreetly employ a new valet for the few days involved, and none the wiser; that Repton, (as he called him), was as fine a rider as any in the country; and that if Miles did not leave to collect the money he, Jeremy, had nothing to lose by spreading the story of Georgina, by devious underhand means, at once. So Miles (who must, anyway, as he privately knew, attempt to speak to the Runners) had agreed with apparent reluctance.

Once mounted again after his hasty meal and galloping with Repton a little to the rear, his thoughts returned to the dilemma of how he was to deceive Repton and speak to the Bow Street Runners secretly. Merely to elude the man, even if this were possible, or to have him detained privately would undoubtedly raise such suspicion, either at once or later, that his elaborate charade of a change of heart in favor of Jeremy would be useless and Georgina's reputation again placed at risk. His town house he knew to be empty save for an old couple left there as caretakers. The man was slow though honest and thorough, but his wife was sharp-witted as a needle. Miles mused: perhaps he could somehow manage to send a message to Captain Whittaker (and so to the Runners) through her; perhaps, indeed, he thought with a sudden flash of inspiration, they could be persuaded to pose as his bankers! For although he had incorrectly represented to Jeremy his credit as standing so badly with the bank that they would refuse to send a representative up to Lancashire, there would seem to Repton nothing odd, at least, in their sending such a representative the short distance from the bank to Miles's London residence to discuss money matters.

So Miles galloped on, his mind occupied with his plans, and so Repton rode close behind, all his thoughts concentrated on how to keep his quarry constantly in view until the return to Lancashire. Neither of them, therefore, noticed a small unobtrusive creature, dressed in a shabby, old-fashioned, full-skirted coat, and an even shabbier beaver, who rode as far behind as possible without losing them; who stopped—at a distance—when they stopped; and rode on when they did. Even if both men had not been so occupied with their thoughts, there was little to attract their attention to such a nonentity. Except that he rode a very fine horse and paid well for an equally good animal whenever he changed mounts.

It was dusk the following day when Miles finally arrived with Repton at his London house; the lamplighters had already been at work (for here and there were gas lights in the modern fashion), and the shutters were up. Prolonged pounding on the heavy front door eventually produced the

caretaker, horrified to find his master and a new valet re-
quiring entrance; close behind the old servant was his wife,
clucking with concern about beds and food. Miles calmed
them both, reassured them that, as no messenger had been
sent, they could scarcely be expected to be prepared for
him, and agreed to wine, hot soup, and some dressed
mutton, which was all they could produce, while beds
were made ready. He was amused to find Repton gave him
no chance to speak with either servant alone, but he had
expected this, and had contrived, while refreshing himself
at the last inn, to pen a hasty note to his ex-Guardee friend,
asking him to speak to Mr. James Read of Bow Street
urgently on his behalf about an unspecified serious matter,
and requesting that two responsible Runners disguised
as bankers be sent to Miles's house well before noon next
day. He explained he was watched constantly, and this
was the only safe method of communication.

How he was to get the caretaker's wife even to take the
note from him Miles knew not; nor whether, if he did so, it
would reach Captain Whittaker. There had been no chance
to seal it with a wafer, and he would have to depend merely
on the Captain's name and direction on the outside of the
folded paper.

The only consolation, Miles reflected, as he and Repton
ate the hastily prepared meal and drank the wine before
retiring, was that the woman was loyal, sharp, and (unlike
her husband) able to read. If he could contrive . . . As
Repton bent his head to the last of his mutton, Miles raised
his eyebrows at the caretaker's wife, who was waiting at
table as best she could, and allowed her a glimpse of the
folded sheet of paper in his crumpled napkin, before he

threw this down and announced himself ready to retire to bed. It was the best he could do. Perhaps during the night, some other plan would occur to him. For he certainly would not sleep, any more, he suspected, than his watch dog would. Despite the recently lit fire, his huge bedchamber was still damp and cold; and he noted, without surprise, the truckle bed that Repton, as a faithful valet, had succeeded in having installed in the adjoining dressing room.

Next morning, however, revealed another example of the quick wits of the Cockney. The caretaker's wife, producing a rather meager breakfast, informed Miles, with a high color and a private wide stare, that she had sent the boy from the street barrow at the corner to collect some vegetables and meat, which should arrive as quickly as might be. She hoped she had done right, there being nothing in the house, and nobody to do any marketing at present. If it had not been for that stare, Miles would have taken the statement at its face value, as Repton certainly did. As it was, however, he guessed her to refer to the message and thanked her calmly. Then, handing her a sealed note to his bankers (which he had penned asking them to call after noon or later, taking care to have Repton looking over his shoulder as he did so), he told her, with an equally wide stare, to have her husband go with the message to the bank.

But he had spoken haughtily, overbearingly, which was not in character, for he was invariably courteous with his servants—only Repton was not to know this. And as, at the same time, he had given her a further stare and an unobtrusive shake of his head, he was fairly certain she would take his meaning and not send the second missive. He then sat back to hope for the best and await developments, telling himself that, at worst, he would have two sets of bankers, false earlier in the morning, and genuine somewhat later, on his hands.

They came toward eleven o'clock. Three sober-looking men, two dark-suited, heavy-jowled, with pompous expressions, the third funereally clad also, but tall, thin, with a rather military air about him. The caretaker's wife, with another expressionless look, announced 'some gennulmen from the bank, sir,' and then withdrew. The two Bow Street Runners, and the ex-Guardee (who had obviously and irrepressibly come along to see what was afoot and who gave no hint whatsoever of knowing Miles) bowed and advanced, with all the disapproving air of "Cits" for the ramshackle, profligate aristocracy, into the long, dark library. Miles, rising, held out his hand to the tallest, thinnest, and seemingly most intimidating of the three, saying courteously,

"How good of you to come in person, sir! And at so early an hour, too! I can only hope you will all oblige me in this matter."

Captain Whittaker, not a whit put out and with the cold eye that had looked dispassionately, and of necessity, on so many campaigns and massacres in the Peninsula War, now stared icily at Miles, saying, with a twirl of his mustache (perhaps a shade too military),

"That remains to be seen, sir. However, I should wish to introduce Mr. Read, who is second only to myself, and his chief clerk. Now, to business."

Miles, looking, he hoped, suitably anxious, seated the

visitors round a heavy library table, and then ordered Repton to bring wine and biscuits, "For I feel sure you would like some refreshment, gentlemen."

Repton, impressed, unsuspicious, his guard now justifiably relaxed, went away, as a good valet, to collect this, thus giving Miles time to warn his visitors against him; and made no demur when, having returned with the refreshment, he was superciliously ordered by the 'chief banker' to retire again from the room. After the doors had closed on him, the man introduced as Mr. Read got up lightly, considering his rather heavy build and, walking over to the ornate doors, reopened them carefully: the long, wide corridor outside was empty.

"Well, your watchdog, as you referred to him just now, has gone, Mr. Barrett. So perhaps you will be so good as to explain what all this is about? Our mutual friend here," indicating Captain Whittaker, "vouches absolutely for you, and assures me you are not given to unnecessary starts and alarums."

A little disliking the speaker's manner, but aware that, after all, he had had to come some distance, to oblige a friend certainly, but at the request of a man he did not know, to discuss he knew not what, Miles said quietly,

"Briefly, I must tell you that I suspect a Luddite rising in an area that has long been quiet. But I think it will serve our purpose better if I first ask you a question regarding a trouble-maker you attempted, unsuccessfully, to apprehend some years ago, in Yorkshire."

He then told them what he knew of Jeremy Tregannan's suspected past history and asked if they or any of their confreres could augment it in any way. Above all, whether they had any likeness, as was sometimes made, of the man sought in the southeastern affair, supposing he had ever been held in jail, perhaps for questioning, or disturbing the peace.

As he was speaking, the so-called clerk to the bank, in fact the elder though subordinate of the two Runners, became more and more restless. At last, as Miles paused, he broke into the account, saying,

"I know the man! I wasn't in on it, but I heard all about the inquiry, sir. It interested me. After he was hunted unsuccessfully for inciting to riot down South, and perhaps in French pay, they suspected him of being a Northern trouble-maker as well, as you know. So they had a drawing made by an eyewitness, an old Sussex craftsman—an engraver who had little time for rioting—for one of the Runners to take North to see if they could get anyone to name him or lay information!"

The atmosphere tightened. "They never laid hands on him, of course, neither up there nor in the South. But the likeness is still locked in the general desk, I'll swear. Perhaps I should get it?"

"Later, my dear fellow," said the chief Runner. "Just now, let us have Mr. Barrett finish his tale and his questions. That is, if he has any more."

Miles said flatly, "I refer to the killing of a mill owner of evil repute in Yorkshire: the organizing of that rising, and the killing itself, were attributed to the same man (as your subordinate says) on account of his methods of rabble-rousing, as well as his description?"

"Yes," agreed Mr Read, slowly.

"But, apart from the fact that the murderer could not be

found, there were no actual witnesses to the Northern killing . . . at least, none who would come forward?"

James Read spoke even more slowly. "There must have been witnesses. The place was like a battlefield. But it was night, there was a heavy pall of smoke and, perhaps reasonably, no one liked to accuse another with certainty. Or was afraid to. Several people spoke secretly, however, of *two* men when the murder was done: one close by, an unwilling onlooker . . ."

"So there *was* a witness!" Miles was surprised. The chief Bow Street officer looked at him soberly. "Yes. We kept it secret that we knew of the onlooker, hoping to trap him. But he was never found either. We searched, questioned, held on for a very long time. But that witness was either a friend of the murderer, or bribed, or soon dead. Anyway, as I say, no more was seen of him."

There was a long pause, while each man pondered on things past. At last, James Read observed carefully, "I think as you do, Mr. Barrett, that before we go into details of your present suspected plot, it would be as well to see if your trouble-maker resembles the man we have been speaking of. Fairclough," he turned to his colleague, "I think you had best be off and bring back that sketch if, as you say, you can lay your hands on it. But, we must be careful. . . Mr. Barrett, perhaps you would call your watchdog in on some pretext, and I can instruct my colleague in his hearing to fetch a certain document from the bank. That way, he should have no suspicion."

Accordingly, more wine was called for, and in Repton's presence Fairclough was sent, ostensibly, to the bank. When both men had left the library, however, an uneasy silence fell. Bow Street was, after all, some distance from elegant Mayfair, and those who remained were impatient to know the outcome of the matter. Miles took the opportunity of saying that if the sketch did portray the man he suspected, it might be possible to prevent the uprising utterly, as he knew his whereabouts. But that in the interests of justice, he could not say more at present, for he might, after all, be indicting an innocent man. It was obvious that Mr. Read, like all policemen—and understandably enough—felt Miles was being too nice in the matter. But Miles would say no more: he had his own ideas on how to deal with Jeremy Tregannan and so stop the uprising, for he had also his daughter to consider.

At last, Fairclough returned with what appeared to be a rolled document under his arm. Miles, conscious of a sudden chill, looked down as the sheet was discreetly unrolled: Jeremy Tregannan, younger, a little plumper, but unmistakable, stared back at him.

And there was yet another discovery to come: intermittently, after Repton's earlier appearance with the wine and biscuits, and during the wait for Fairclough to return, a look of intense concentration had passed over Mr. Read's face. Now he said, suddenly, "Roll up that damned likeness, since we've identified it, Fairclough. And if you would be so good, sir, send for that valet of yours again, if you please!"

Miles looked at the speaker curiously. His brow was creased in an effort of recollection, his whole manner dogged and alert.

"Well, we can hardly demand more wine—this is not yet finished! But I can call him in, if you wish, and instruct him to order the caretaker's wife to prepare us something more substantial to eat?"

"That will do excellent well, I thank you."

As Miles walked over to pull the bell he noticed the two Runners in earnest, low-voiced conversation, and a sudden expression of enlightenment on Fairclough's face, as he nodded vigorous confirmation to what was said to him.

So Repton was once more summoned to the library, this time ostensibly to receive instructions for the caretaker's wife. If he was aware of Fairclough's and James Read's hard stares, he did not show it; and anyway, supposing the visitors to be bankers as he did, he had no reason to be apprehensive or overly observant. It came as a shock to him therefore, when James Read said, suddenly,

"Would you extend your left arm, my man?"

Repton's reaction was instantaneous: he put the arm in question behind him, and began to back away swiftly toward the door, his eyes flicking dangerously from side to side, his right hand moving toward the flap of his coat.

But in a flash, Fairclough was to the rear of him, pinioning his right arm up across his back while Read, from the front, grasped his left wrist and held it hard.

Miles, half-risen as had Captain Whittaker, found himself observing a long, thin hand, with the little finger curiously bent across the fourth one, rather in the manner of a hammer toe. And then, as James Read roughly pulled up the coat sleeve of his prisoner, he saw a tattoo revealed on the forearm, livid against the white, curiously hairless, skin. Read, without loosening his grip on his prisoner, glanced at Miles and said with deep satisfaction,

"The missing witness. I saw that deformity when he

carried in the wine, though over the years he has doubtless become skillful at not letting it be obvious! Only we are trained, Mr. Barrett, to observe. . ." He paused and then went on, "It meant nothing to me until just now, I regret to say; it was, after all, several years ago, and many cases have intervened. Only during our recent conversation odd snippets of the investigation we were discussing kept returning to my mind. And I recalled, suddenly, reading the secret deposition of one observer that he saw the witness's arm against the door jamb as he drew back from the smoke and the murder. It was illuminated, for a brief moment, you see, by a new spurt of flame: the hand was deformed in this manner, and there was a tattoo mark on the forearm."

He smiled triumphantly at Repton and added, "We have a signed deposition on it, man! People weren't as nervous of informing against an unknown as against a ringleader, seemingly!"

There was an instant's silence. Then Repton, realizing that he had, despite all his care, been tricked and that these men were not bankers, but the law, jerked furiously toward Miles, shouting obscenities, while his eyes flashed with fury.

A comparatively short while later, a closed carriage drew unobtrusively up to the door of Miles's house, and James Read led Repton, his hands now securely tied behind him, swiftly into the vehicle. Read, in his stolid way, was pleased with himself. As head of the Runners, a body of men to a great extent a law unto themselves anyway, he had come to an agreement with his prisoner: identification of, and testimony against, the man now calling himself Tregannan, and in return, absolute amnesty. But refusal to aid the Runners in this way would result in transport to Botany Bay for past crimes against the Peace of the Realm and for present Conspiracy. Repton felt he had no choice: he had agreed to cooperate.

However, discreet as James Read's departure with his prisoner had been, it was not discreet enough to escape the sharp eyes of the shabby, unobtrusive little man who leant so negligently against the railings at a corner nearby. He had, unfortunately, missed the caretaker's wife's brief conversation with the street barrow boy the previous evening, being engaged in a quick search for a convenient place to keep vigil and avoid the Watch. But today he was not so unfortunate: his long street vigil had paid excellent dividends. With his lips pursed in a soundless whistle of dismay, he made his way hurriedly to the mews where his excellent mount was tethered, and set off, as fast as he could, for Lancashire: Mr. Tregannan was not going to be pleased with his news, that was certain.

Because of his swift departure, he missed seeing Miles leave the house but a little later with the other Runner, both turning their horses hastily towards the Great North Road again, it having been agreed that Miles Barrett and Fairclough should hurry back to Lancashire together, Fairclough to assess the situation as best he could (with Miles's local knowledge), and attempt, by arresting Jeremy Tregannan, to forestall any insurrection. Or, if he felt this not to be possible, to alert the local authorities after all. They had still, of course, no knowledge of the seedy little informer, with his good headstart on them.

Miles spoke little. He had hoped to gain some knowledge from the Runners certainly, but to deal with Jeremy
privately. He had not, in fact, realized how thorough and
efficient this body of men were. Several times he glanced
at the hard, stern profile of his companion. Perhaps if he
could gain the fellow's sympathy, his cooperation . . .
his mind flagged. And when, inevitably, he started to think
again, his thoughts had taken a different direction. He
must remember the safety of many people was at stake; he
could not deflect the course of justice, now so inexorably
and correctly in motion, merely for the sake of his foolish
daughter. His heart ached.

Chapter 19

IN Miles's house, in a bedchamber across from Georgina's,
Thea woke to utter blackness. Something, she knew, some
sound or movement had disturbed her, but now the silence,
like the blackness, was impenetrable again. She turned on
her side and looked across toward the windows (for she
never drew the bed curtains round her at night except in
deepest winter), but to her dismay she recalled seeing that
the heavy window drapes had been closed earlier by one
of the servants. She herself had been too tired, her shoulder
too painful, to reopen them when she had finally said
good-night to Georgina and entered her own room.

Not even a glimmer of moonlight showed through the
thick fabric. Thea lay rigid, her ears straining for the
sound, or whatever it was that had wakened her, certain
in her mine that she had not dreamed it. No! There it was

again! A furtive scrabbling. Outside, on the fabric of the house? She slipped out of bed and, her nightgown floating behind her, ran lightly over to the windows, parted the curtains, silently released the catch to ease up the sash, and leaned cautiously out. If anything had been there, there was nothing now, either below or above her: only the buttressed classical stone heads, two stories up, that were in fact rain spouts, gazed out over the quiet park, ghostly in the pale moonlight. No . . . wait! She peered upward and outward again: surely there was one head too many on the parapet. Even as she realized this, the head, or whatever it was, vanished. There must be someone up there, on the roof! And then her eye caught the thick, twisted wisteria that insinuated its way alongside her window and on upward.

Instinctively, she reached for her robe and then, momentarily, for the bell rope. But something, some sixth sense, as she hoped, caused her to withdraw her hand from the heavy tassel, memories of Georgina's earlier midnight excursions flooding her mind. Discretion might be best. . . She eased open the door of the room opposite: the moon-washed windows, the curtains drawn apart here and facing another direction, revealed Georgina herself peacefully asleep, her dark hair neatly braided, her hand under her cheek. Shutting the door soundlessly, Thea cast a glance along the wide carpeted gallery towards the closed door at the far end. This, she knew from rambling once with Georgina, opened into a small vestibule, and then to the back stairs leading to the last two upper floors of the house. If her memory served her right, this wing of the top floor was but attic storage space, and the floor below scarcely used. The servants slept elsewhere in the great house. Moreover, these stairs were the only means of access to the upper floors in this wing, no corresponding backstairs descending on the other side. The intruder, whoever he was, surely could have had no time, so far, to descend them without meeting her.

She began to climb them rapidly therefore, grateful for the faint light which filtered through small uncurtained windows at regular intervals and, arriving at the top, stood gazing the length of a cold, narrow, low-ceilinged corridor that ran into utter blackness to her right, where the faint window light failed to penetrate.

There was no sound, no movement. Feeling foolish now, for, after all, there might be various other ways into the house from the roof, she began to creep uncertainly, past closed doors, towards the blackness ahead, her mind still busy with the fact that, all the same, it must have been up the wisteria, past her bedroom windows, that the intruder had come: those furtive, scuffling noises proved it. And that therefore these stairs were indeed his quickest way down again *inside* the house. . . . But perhaps the intruder was not looking for the quickest way down, or the nearest, as she had instinctively assumed, to Georgina's room: perhaps he had other designs! She should have pulled the bell rope in her room and raised the alarm. He might be contemplating burglary—the house was packed with treasures; or searching for firearms—the gun room was well stocked; or . . . with the word "firearms," her thoughts leaped to insurrection . . . preparing to commit arson or worse!

The horror of these alternatives froze her mind and took her momentarily completely off guard. She was suddenly aware of a muted thump as some part of the ceiling, so it seemed, was flung back, and then a storm lantern from an open trap door above her flashed full on her upturned face. Behind it, an unidentifiable shape crouched and then, at sight of her, gave a furious ejaculation and, leaving the lantern above, leaped forward and down, a swirling mass of dark cloak and clutching hands.

Thea had not time to struggle effectively, though she bit and scratched with a fury that amazed herself. She was overborne, forced flat to the floor, and then felt her head momentarily raised, to be banged smartly on the bare, dusty boards, where, in a sharp many-colored flash, she lost consciousness. But in that split second of having her head raised she glimpsed, in the wavering light of the lantern teetering on the trap door's edge, the wild, contorted features of Jeremy Tregannan, all urbanity gone, and a feverish insane glitter in his eyes.

Thea thought she could not have lost consciousness for long. She still felt warm, her limbs were not stiff, and she recalled, strangely in the circumstances, a heavy fall from a horse in childhood days and the doctor saying laughingly that brainy she might be, but she was, all the same, blessed with a very thick skull . . . Above her, the trap door remained open to a pale patch of night sky; she struggled to her feet, and began to stumble, awkwardly, (aware, suddenly, from the excruciating pain in her shoulder, that it must have been further wrenched in the attack) toward the staircase at the end of the corridor.

Two floors down again, she ran, still following her instincts, to Georgina's room. The door was open, and one glance within showed that Georgina was gone. But not willingly, this time, by the look of it. The bedclothes had been dragged to the ground, and the bed curtains hung drunkenly; a chair lay overturned by the door. Thea rushed to the bell pull and tugged violently, then stumbled off along the corridor to the main staircase.

Chapter 20

THE Runner Fairclough and Miles Barrett, riding hard, saw the blaze of lights from Miles's house as they breasted the last hill, where the road snaked down to the great entrance gates of the estate. Even as they momentarily reined in, appalled, more lights, torches, tapers, sprang up, and figures could be seen hurrying, seemingly pointlessly, to and fro both within and without the building. Wordlessly, the two riders urged their beasts even faster, and Miles was first to reach the main door and see Thea on the wide, curved steps beneath the huge portico, organizing more men with torches to search the grounds, and apparently speeding Thomas and Miles's chief groom on a journey.

For a brief second, at the sight of Miles, Thea clung to him, her body, in its flimsy night-dress covered only by her heavy dressing gown, tense against him, so that his arms went round her, his desire to comfort her almost stifling him. But then, pulling away suddenly, she made haste to explain what had occurred: Georgina had been abducted, and that but recently, by Jeremy Tregannan.

"He must be on horseback or hiding up, Miles. The gates were all closed and barred for the night, and the lodgekeeper swears no vehicle got through!"

There was no time for further words: Miles and the Runner turned their attention to organizing the more distant hunt for Tregannan and his captive, leaving Thea, at her own insistence and now with Thomas's aid, to instruct the indoor servants and estate hands, in continuing to search the house and its environs.

At the gates to the estate Miles and Fairclough reined in, as Miles frowned, considering.

"There are but two routes he could take from here: east, toward the heights, with their natural hiding places, rough tracks, and folk who mind their own counsel; or west, toward the forest. If he turns west, he may well succeed, while we hesitate here, to gain the main highway, and then . . . well, all is up with us, for he has a choice of the highway running North or South, let alone byways."

"You know the terrain, sir," replied Fairclough. "Choose your route. I'll take the other one."

"Right! I shall turn toward the heights and Yorkshire: I know the area, and the people. They'll talk to me. And you, Fairclough, you ride down toward the forest. But if you gain the main highway with no sight of him, turn back, I beg you, and follow my direction for I don't think, yet, he can have got farther than that. And anyway, you shouldn't, at that rate, be too far behind me. It's my belief, you know, that he won't risk the more populated main road, but will attempt to join his sympathizers in Yorkshire!"

And so the two parted. Miles galloped on the lower reaches of the rough road, his new mount's hooves muffled by soft mud (for a drizzle had now set in), his ears alert. Then, gradually, he began to mount, scars overhung him among the soft earth, and the track, strewn now with stones and small rocks, narrowed steadily. His fears for his daughter grew; one could only hope that Tregannan, too, knew the treachery of this alternately greenly smiling, then bleak, terrain.

On an impulse, Miles reined in. And then, scarcely able to believe his ears he heard, on the light wind, first a faint, febrile scream, cut short, then a wild whinny as if from some terrified, or overridden beast. Forcing himself to remain motionless, and not rush blindly in the direction of the sounds he had heard, Miles stroked the arched neck of his mount, willing it to silence. Then, suddenly, the gleaming head tossed up and simultaneously, to the left and above him, he heard, faintly, the regular strumming of hooves on turf. Urging his own mount now to a trot, Miles made his way on up the dangerous track, known from childhood, that wound its perilous way to a treacherous grassy plateau, edged by an escarpment, and thence on to the highest ridges of the desolate scars and fells. So the fugitive must be attempting to make for his Yorkshire allies. Miles prayed again, fervently, that Tregannan, too, knew his route. Cautiously, holding not only his beast, but his mounting impatience in check, he climbed on, his horse picking its footholds delicately. The soft thud of hooves, recently heard, seemed fainter again; yet, as Miles knew, the track he was taking was probably the quickest route to reach his quarry—if, indeed, it were his quarry he had heard. Even of that he was not certain. He gritted his teeth and, giving his mount its head, continued his way cautiously on upward, hidden from above by the swell of hill and rocky outcrop.

At last the grassy plateau was reached. Then suddenly, reining in, both to let his mount regain its breath, and to study the surroundings, Miles heard a wild thunder of hooves, and across his vision hurtled Jeremy Tregannan mounted on a sweat-stained black gelding, making off at breakneck speed into the straggly copse along the spine of the hill ahead, a figure (surely Georgina's) flung limply across his saddle. The fool would break his neck against a branch! Or worse, plunge to his death where the tattered trees ended suddenly in a further outcrop of rocks and boulders, with a steep drop to the valley beneath. That Tregannan had seen Miles was unmistakable. But Miles's warning, shouted hoarsely, remained either ignored or unheard. Miles himself, making a lightning decision, turned his mount and rode, faster than was safe, diagonally across the treacherous ground toward the trees, hoping against hope to head his quarry off his suicidal course. But he was too late. When he was within less than ten yards of the spot he feared, Jeremy erupted from the copse, lying low along the horse's neck, still whipping it to a gallop: his mount sensed the drop instinctively, before its master, and pulling up, stiff-legged, attempted to regain its balance, nostrils flaring. It succeeded, but the jolt of its stopping

unseated Jeremy: over the horse's head he went, downward, bouncing from outcrop to loose rock, from rock to
bush, to end crumpled on a narrow shelf halfway down the
stony precipice. The limp burden he had carried on the
saddle, meanwhile, had slithered inertly down from the
terrified horse's neck into a huddle between its hooves.

Miles, coaxing the beast to remain still, fearing any
minute a kick that would be poor Georgina's quietus,
approached carefully, then bent to drag the inert figure
clear. It was indeed Georgina, alabaster pale, her eyes
closed, her hands and feet bound. With infinite gentleness, he pushed away the cloak's hood from her forehead,
where the hair clung in damp tendrils, loosed her bonds,
and attempted to restore some life into the still figure,
while examining her as well as he could for any injuries.
To the best of his knowledge, he found no bones broken,
but she would not waken. Indeed, her swoon was terrify-
ingly deep; and it was, anyway, impossible to know what
internal injuries she, or her unborn child, had sustained.
Anxiously, he looked about him, aware of a few feeble
cries for help from the hidden ledge of the escarpment, and
at the same time overcome with apprehension for his
daughter's well-being. Either way, he needed help. Making a sudden decision, he remounted and rode some way
back on his tracks until he could see far down below: to
his relief, he could discern Fairclough and two of the men
from his own estate, mounted, gazing anxiously upward.

They made a simple stretcher for Georgina, and Fairclough and one of the men carried her, gently, on the
home-made hurdle, down the tracks to the road, where
others, quickly warned by the second man, riding hard for

home, were already bringing up a light carriage. Miles, aware now that that there was no further immediate help he could give her, that Thea and Mrs. Horrocks would surely summon medical aid and do all they should for her, and that Fairclough, unaware of Jeremy's earlier calls for help, felt his immediate business was to ask questions below, turned his attention to Tregannan, silent now, perhaps dead, so precariously balanced on the narrow ledge, halfway down the cruel precipice. Men had already been told to return with rope in order to raise him. But for the present, with no rope as yet available, Miles began to descend inch by inch, feeling carefully for foot- and handholds, his strong muscles taking the strain slowly, steadily, to the aid of his erstwhile enemy.

Arrived at last, he edged round gingerly until his back was to the sheer face of the precipice, and then knelt carefully to examine the victim, hoping, for Georgina's sake, to find him dead already. At first he seemed not to be breathing; but then he stirred faintly, and his pulse flickered. Miles said softly, "Jeremy, time enough for our differences later. Help is on the way, but can I do aught for you now? Where are you hurt, do you know?"

There was no reaction until, suddenly, the opaque, sloe-colored eyes opened fractionally, then further, little by little, until they stared wide, unseeing, into Miles's own. Then, like a shifting backcloth in a play, they slipped uncannily into focus, sheer, undying hatred in their depths.

"I want no help of *you!* I prefer to die! You and your easy good nature, your careless care for your tenants! Life's just a game to you! You have no ideals, no causes at heart! So it is *you* who are maimed, not I! Inwardly!"

The voice, which had begun so venomously, faded suddenly. The eyelids fluttered over the erstwhile fierce eyes.

Miles, touched despite himself, said gently, "You misjudge me, Tregannan. I do have ideals . . . causes, if you will . . . only my remedies are different from yours . . . but just now I have only one aim, to recover you to safety!"

"For what? To die by hanging? I thank you, but no!" Jeremy Tregannan took a deep shuddering breath, and went on, "I had rather die now. While my revenge is sweet, knowing your daughter is dying too!"

In the horrified pause, his voice dragged on. "I had you and Repton followed to London without his knowledge, either. Poor Repton was arrested, yes. But I was warned by my man who followed you both. So when I had the news from him, I put in hand that which I knew would hurt you most; far, far more than any insurrection: I abducted your precious daughter! It should not have taken long . . . I had a mount tethered outside your wall. Time enough to organize the Luddites to arms afterwards, albeit without those firearms! But my wretched luck ran out! All the same, your daughter *has* been abducted, and by now, I suppose, must be dead! Or if not yet, then as good as! All that jolting, like a sack, athwart my horse, in her condition!" His grimace was like a death's head.

Miles gripped his hands together. He said, slowly, deliberately dispassionate, "I do not know how she fares . . . but for your treason, your self-interest . . ."

He got no further. The injured man somehow raised himself on his elbow, his sneer now a rictus in his dying face,

"No treason! No self-interest! I am a Luddite . . . and I speak, I *fight* only for the rights of the oppressed! I will . . . not . . . accept . . . your . . . charity in attempting to save me . . . for the gallows, like as not, anyway!" And even as he spoke, even before Miles could move, Jeremy Tregannan had hurled himself onto his side and over the ledge of the precipice, to fall, grimly soundless, spread-eagled, onto the boulders of the valley below.

Chapter 21

As soon as she reasonably could, Thea left Thomas in charge of the local search parties and hurried back to her bedchamber to dress more warmly. She had scarcely done throwing a thick scarf-shawl around the shoulders of one of her warmest gowns when a hesitant tap on the door revealed a little maid with large apprehensive eyes, and a message that a woman was at the back door of the house and anxious to speak with her; indeed, had been so insistent there was no putting her off.

"What sort of woman?"

"A . . . *person*, miss. At the *kitchen* door," came the answer, with all the snobbishness of the age and the little servant's upbringing in the Big House.

"Well, you had best lead me to her then, my dear,"

said Thea, bustling the diminutive figure ahead of her in the direction of the servants' quarters.

Arrived in the large, square, scrubbed kitchen, neat even on such a night as this had turned out to be, Thea had no difficulty in recognizing Mrs. Schofield, impatient as ever, certainly agitated, her black shoe-button eyes snapping with anxiety. Her curtsy to Thea was of the briefest, and casting a glance round the kitchen, at the wide-eyed little maid and a loitering footman, she said at once,

"We can't speak here, miss, if it please you. Somewhere quiet it must be!"

Wordlessly, Thea led the way through the heavy baize door and along the corridor to the library, which she rightly judged to be empty at such a time. She drew her unexpected visitor toward the fire, which still burned, though low at this hour, and, indicating a chair nearby, seated herself opposite. Mrs. Schofield wasted no time,

"I am come to warn you, Miss Langham. The so-called gentleman you spoke of came riding demented to our cottage but an hour or so ago, roused my husband from sleep, and ordered him to make at once for what he called 'the house' and tell them that was there that he had been delayed, but that they was to wait for him, as he had some personal business, that yet affected their plans, to attend to first, and that he would be with them within a short while."

"And did your husband understand the message?"

Mrs. Schofield took no offense, since obviously none was meant. "Oh yes, miss, and remembered it. He was made to repeat it, you see, several times. And as it happened, he knew from Mick that the leaders were to gather there at the house tonight." Mrs. Schofield paused, then continued very low,

"They didn't either of them know I heard—I pretended to be asleep, you see, and I never came near when all this whispering went on in the parlor . . . I hid behind t'door to stairs!"

"So what you are saying is, the ringleaders are assembled in this one place and ripe for the picking?"

"That, miss, yes! But also that Mr. Barrett and his friends had best be quick if they mean to have them: Sam's just returned with a tale that the ringleaders, some of them not from these parts, *is* all assembled, but Mr. Tregannan's not joined them yet, and they're becoming impatient, fearing a trap!" She added, somewhat shamefacedly, "I couldn't come earlier, on account of Sam being took among them, you'll understand, miss, although I know you'd have done your best for him. But it's certain sure the ringleaders'll be gone soon, I reckon; and with them, every chance of catching them red-handed and stopping any rising!" She looked at Thea's worried countenance and finished urgently,

"I *beg* you, Miss, if you want to avoid bloodshed, get Mr. Barrett to move *now*. If he rounds up the ringleaders and makes it known at once that he's done so, the rank and file will just melt away. You know yourself," she added, with utter contempt in her voice, "the silly sheep won't stir if the dogs aren't there to bundle them together and drive them on!"

Thea, not pausing to wonder that Mrs. Schofield was so familiar with the names of both Tregannan and Miles, said tautly, "Mr. Barrett is not here. He is, I fear, on the trail of Jeremy Tregannan, and God knows where that has led him at this moment! Perhaps even to 'the house' itself, as you call it!" Her heart contracted at the thought, and the two women gazed at each other in consternation, their minds busy.

At last Mrs. Schofield, less occupied with fears for Miles Barrett's safety, and perhaps attributing more power to Thea than she in fact possessed, continued desperately, "*Please,* Miss, you *must* do something! If these men are caught and dealt with by gentlemen such as Mr. Barrett, we can all go back to living peacefully again! No hangings for us ordinary folk, no deportations or floggings! And no more trouble! I *swear* it. The women will see to that, watch their menfolk if need be—at least watch the hotheads among them, and that's all that's needed! They realize, the women, that rioting and suchlike solves nothing, only brings more troubles, less food, misery untold!" She finished briefly, urgent for Thea's immediate cooperation.

"They've learnt, you see. Bitterly. At first, some of them backed their men. But when it came to being forced to stay indoors with their little ones while the secret meetings went on, and talk of the Frenchies and a bloody revolution, and going in fear of their persons, if they didn't agree—*and* all the tavern visits, well, they learned sense! That their men were like big louts playing at war— and not even knowing they were being *used!*"

Thea, seeing remembered distress in the prematurely lined face, said gently, "I understand." But Mrs. Schofield scarcely heard her, being still occupied with her recent struggle to gain at least the women's support.

"We all saw you, you know, the women, that time when you came so bedraggled down the fellside. Some of us knew you for a well-intentioned woman, not daft, haughty, like so many of your kind, and we thought—a few of us —that you would help if you could." She paused, and then added, "Only I was so afeard the men might see me that day, or one of the hotter-headed women . . ."

"But now?"

"Now, I am here, to speak openly, for the women. Urgently, while there's still time! To ask for Mr. Barrett and his like to help save our menfolk from following a blind cause blindly. To say they realize now that the Frenchies may be involved, or other revolutionaries! Nor we don't want the official authorities, neither, for they're cumbersome at best, and with them, we'll *all* suffer!"

Thea nodded, absently, her mind frantically busy.

"This 'house,' is it the deserted cottage in a copse, some miles to the west of Lord Barton's estate?"

"Yes. It's a rallying point, miss. Seems they assemble and make plans and things there. According to Mick . . ."

Inconsequentially, Thea's mind flew to the unusual secret drawer that by merest chance she knew how to open.

"How many organizers—leaders—are there, do you know?"

"Six, seven? No, I can only guess."

Thea sighed. "I think we shall have to inform the authorities, you know. I agree it is urgent. And anyway, there is a Runner up here already. Also, we have no way of ascertaining when Mr. Barrett—" She broke off to add, as the thought struck her, "Or perhaps I could send to Lord Barton! He is a compassionate man, too, Mrs. Schofield, and a . . . tactful . . . one!"

"Aye. Good with his tenantry too . . ." Mrs Schofield looked up hopefully.

But at this moment all thought of rounding up the ringleaders was temporarily banished from Thea's mind by the arrival of the carriage containing Georgina, now half-conscious, crying out incoherently, and of a waxlike pallor that frightened all who saw it. Deliberately on Thea's part, for discretion's sake, Mrs. Schofield was abandoned firmly, though with promise of a speedy return, in the library. The housekeeper, Mrs. Horrocks, and Thea herself carried Georgina into her bedchamber, while Thomas was ordered to send one trusty man with an urgent discreet written message to Dr. Gordon in the village; and another to Lord Barton, requesting his immediate presence secretly, armed and with some stalwart servants, on a matter of the nation's safety.

Once laid down on her bed, to Thea and Mrs. Horrock's horror, Georgina's agony grew worse. The crying out increased, her consciousness returning rapidly, while she writhed on the covers, her hands constantly plucking at her stomach, her back arching spasmodically. The two women looked gravely at one another, the only question in their minds, would the doctor come in time to save the sufferer, if not to avoid a miscarriage. Meanwhile, Thea, ignorant in such matters, did as Mrs. Horrocks instructed her, and prayed through her teeth for the life of the young creature in such agony before her.

Within a very short time, however, Dr. Gordon arrived, and Miles Barrett only a little later. All entry to the sick room was, of necessity, barred except for the doctor, Thea, and the housekeeper, but before returning there, Thea, holding Miles's hands in her firm grip, said urgently that he must not worry; that Dr. Gordon, an excellent, competent doctor as he knew, had said there was no immediate danger to Georgina's life; and that she herself would remain with Georgina constantly. She then, of necessity, spoke of Mrs. Schofield, so impatiently immured in the library, and of the news she had brought. Miles, his tired eyes red-rimmed, his face taut with shock, listened to what she had to say, then told her as gently as possible, of Jeremy's deliberate death. He added quietly,

"He was mad, Thea. Obsessed. Of that I am convinced. Consumed by his hatred of frequently harmless people and his bitter desire for revenge against the system that had, however indirectly, robbed him of his patron. He might, I suppose, have been a Paineite or a Jacobin. But I think not . . . anyway, we shall probably never really be certain now."

At this moment, perhaps fortunately, Lord Barton arrived, armed, and accompanied by his chief groom and several loyal men, quite mystified at Thea's cryptic summons, but determined to obey it without question. So Thea escorted Miles and William Barton to Mrs. Schofield, thinking, as she did so, that it was as well the extreme urgency of the rebel situation and Miles's natural sense of duty should take possession of him. Otherwise, with only Georgina's well-being to occupy his thoughts, he might, perhaps, have run temporarily mad. Sighing, she turned to the staircase again.

Chapter 22

SOME weeks later, Thea sat at the long, beautiful Georgian windows in that same bedchamber in Miles's house which she had occupied during the eventful night of Jeremy Tregannan's death. All was peaceful. The sun, setting across the hills, flooded the sky blood red; it gave lurid illumination to the hayricks in the low sloping fields below the ridge, and cast ever-lengthening shadows downward to the meadows and to the farm houses huddled against their barns. She shuddered, a sudden image of those same ricks fired, blazing, crossed her imagination; she visualized dark, crazed silhouttes of men against the skyline, moving along the ridge perhaps, then breaking apart, eddying, pouring like water towards the huddled farm buildings, and heard in her mind the dreadful clang

217

of metal on wood as barn doors were stormed, and new threshing machines shattered. She imagined a farmer, perhaps, remonstrating, then the sudden flash of a musket shot, or a heavy blow with a farm implement mowing him down, and heard the wild yell as his buildings, too, were set ablaze.

She rose abruptly, out of patience with herself for pictures in her mind that had no foundation in reality, in this part of the world at least. For the Bow Street Runner Fairclough, along with Miles Barrett and William Barton and a few discreet loyal followers, had overpowered the group of ringleaders assembled in the secret house, taking them by surprise. They had found incriminating documents regarding marked mills, factories, and farms, too, in the secret drawer Thea had earlier discovered, and now all instigators of the uprising (all, that is, but Jeremy Tregannan) were awaiting trial in the jails of Lancashire and Yorkshire whence they had come, along with the firearms dealer, forced to yield up his hidden cache.

However, being a sensible man, and in accord with Miles Barrett and William Barton in this matter, Fairclough, empowered by his own not inconsiderable Bow Street authority, had professed no interest in the rank and file of the would-be insurrection, the tools of these ringleaders; and anyway the local insurgents themselves had melted away like snow. No one knew aught of any plot, no one informed, and there the matter rested. In brief, the uprising was over before it had even begun, and peace still reigned throughout the county.

All the same, Thea's mind still could not rest. She glanced away over the hills, visualizing mills and factories now, strung out beyond her in the sad, spoiled, swiftly changing countryside, and heard in her mind the heavy march of feet, the rag-tag and bobtail of humanity, the fanatic alongside the honest artisan, marching grimly to mill and foundry gates, to shout threats and bang with staves against the railings. Or saw them standing in silence, stolid, resentful, until a sudden yell, or a speech of defiance from inside the building, or the chance discharge of a musket from loyal militia perhaps, reminded the marchers of their very real grievances and impelled them to action. Such things had occurred once here, but would not, please God, happen again. All the same, what of these people, ill-paid, suffering, and now often desperate? Would they gain any redress, any help in their hard, bitter struggle for survival? She could at least find out what could be done among her father's influential friends, and with Miles's help, too. . . .

A sudden scratching at the door broke the trend of her thoughts. The nurse Dr. Gordon had sent for stood there, her kind but rather florid features wreathed in smiles.

"Miss Georgina is asking for you, ma'am, if you would be so good."

Thea, glad to be distracted from her morbid imaginings, smiled and rose at once, making her way across the corridor to the chamber opposite.

In her large, ornate bed, Georgina looked frail, unreal as a wax doll. Since losing her child she had lost weight too, with terrible swiftness, so that she began to be despaired of, until about a week ago. Then, suddenly, so the doctor and nurse opined, she was on the mend. Today, she even smiled at her visitor, and Thea, delighted at the improvement, at the absence of that dreadful listlessness and inertia, smiled back, taking Georgina's hand as she did so. Really, she reflected, stroking the soft curls, the loss of the child was perhaps for the best; the matter had been kept very close, Jeremy Tregannan was dead, and no one, save those immediately around her, who loved her, would ever know what had befallen Georgina. Dr. Gordon, too, would be professionally silent, and had even been so cautious as to send for a nurse from London, one whose discretion was boundless. "There are more of these cases than you can imagine," he had said grimly at the time, "and we are of necessity prepared for such!" So, with good fortune, Georgina should improve now, fast; and soon be able to take up her normal life again, little by little. She might even, indeed, be well enough to attend her dearest friend Lucy's marriage to that rather dull son of the choleric, retired naval officer. Or, if this were thought to prove too great a strain too soon, she could at least visit with them when more fully recovered.

Thea's generous mouth widened into a smile: at least Georgina would be sufficiently recovered to be a bridesmaid at Thea's own wedding, planned now for late autumn. The smile still on her lips, she turned as the door opened to admit Miles, and with one hand still in Georgina's, held out the other to her lover. Miles bent his tall, straight back, and taking her outstretched hand in his own strong ones, kissed first the palm, then the fingers one by one, with great gentleness.